HELEN'S SOUTHERN COMFORT

Brett D. Elfenbein

THE *Erotic* Print Society
London 2003

THE *Erotic* Print Society
EPS, 1 Maddox Street
LONDON W1S 2PZ

Tel (UK only): 0800 026 25 24
Fax: +44 (0)20 7437 3528
Email: eros@eroticprints.org
Web: www.eroticprints.org

© 2003 MacHo Ltd, London UK

ISBN : 1-898998-71-X

HELEN'S SOUTHERN COMFORT

Brett D. Elfenbein

THE *Erotic* Print Society

Foreword

The history of erotic literature has always been clandestine, and, apart from furtive purchases of under-the-counter hardcore, American readers between the end of the war and the mid-1960s could only openly buy paperbacks with lurid covers that always promised, like first dates, far more than they actually delivered. However, the sale of two trashy paperbacks at a news-stand in New York's Times Square was to change the history of erotic publishing in the United States forever.

Previously there had been several landmark cases involving the publication of books that extended the boundaries of what was legally acceptable. These included James Joyce's *Ulysses*, D.H. Lawrence's *Lady Chatterley's Lover*, Henry Miller's *Tropic of Cancer*, John Cleland's *Memoirs of a Woman of Pleasure* and William Burrough's *Naked Lunch*. All novels which today we celebrate and study as major works of literature.

The pivotal moment came when Robert Redrup, a Times Square newsstand clerk, sold two pulp sex novels, *Lust Pool* and *Shame Agent* to plain-clothes policeman, for which he was tried and convicted in 1965.

William Hamling, who published the books under his Nightstand imprint in San Diego, paid Redrup's legal bills to the Supreme Court and the resulting case, *Redrup v. New York* in May 1967, truly opened the floodgates of what was acceptable.

Hamling, and his lawyer Stanley Fleishman, firmly believed that he was not selling, as was said about his books, "commercialised obscenity," nor would he admit to "titillating the prurient interests of people with a weakness for such expression." Hamling felt his books were giving people who would never have the skills to read and enjoy *Ulysses*, *Fanny Hill* or *Naked Lunch* what they wanted.

The judge presiding over the case of Redrup, Justice Potter Stewart, went far beyond his established just-left-of-centre position on obscenity to the most radical of outlooks. Apparently the vote to affirm Ralph Ginzburg's conviction for his magazine *Eros* was his personal wake-up call. In his Ginzburg summary Stewart wrote:

Censorship reflects a society's lack of confidence in itself. It is a hallmark of an authoritarian regime. Long ago those who wrote our First Amendment charted a different course. They believed a society can be truly strong only when it is truly free. In the realm of expression they put their faith, for better or worse, in the enlightened choice of the people, free from the interference of a policeman's intrusive thumb or a judge's heavy hand. So it is that the Constitution protects coarse expression as well as refined, and vulgarity no less than elegance. A book worthless to me may convey something of value to my neighbour. In the free society to which our Constitution has committed us, it is for each to choose for himself.

Stewart's arguments were persuasive enough to convince the court to reverse Redrup's original conviction by 7-2. This decision by the United States Supreme Court affirmed that consenting adults ought to be constitutionally entitled, under the First Amendment, to acquire and read any publication that they wished, including those agreed to be obscene or pornographic, free of interference from the U.S. Government.

Under this guiding principle the Supreme Court adopted a policy of systematically reversing without further opinion ("Redruping") all obscenity convictions which reached it. Scores of obscenity rulings involving paperback sex books, girlie magazines and peep shows were overturned.

Despite an attempt to reverse the tide of pornography by new Chief Justice Warren E. Burger in the 1970s an explosion in paperback publishing followed. Carpet-bagger publishers burst into life across America, including Brandon House, Essex House, Lancer, Midwood, Pendulum, Pleasure Readers and many others. Every aspect of human sexuality was covered in a sexual anarchy of threesomes, foursomes and more-somes in every combination of genders and colours, often including the whole family, their pets and assorted farm animals to boot. Every genre was exploited from incest to Nazi sex with everything in-between in a total assault on the values of bourgeois culture. One can imagine publishers and authors sitting in bars coming up with titles in alcohol-and dope-fuelled brainstorming sessions which would then be commissioned out to a stable of jobbing hacks for around $200 a book.

Past Venus Press will reissue the highlights from this post-Redrup period, many of which were originally considered to have had no literary merit whatsoever and to be utterly without redeeming social importance. But that, of course, was part of their charm.

MICHAEL GOSS

Prelude

The great river rolled gently between the dense vegetation on its banks, like some huge animal: a little sluggish, perhaps, but very much alive. Tall, graceful hardwoods, their branches dripping Spanish moss, towered over lesser trees which in turn overshadowed the thick bushes and shrubs that overhung the river's banks. What had roared high in the southern tip of the mighty Appalachian range as a fresh, clean mountain torrent now made it's stately progress through the riverlands of Georgia, its waters opaque and murky.

The broad waterway's banks swarmed with life; birds flitted from tree to tree, their plumage flashing in the smoky light; occasionally a splash or a flurry of activity would signal the presence of a predator. Nature carried on her grim dance of survival at every level: the sweet, cloying odour of rotting vegetation, the stink of decomposing carrion, the gaseous emanations of the mud banks and neighbouring swamps all hung heavily in the air that gradually thickened in the long days of summer heat. Human detritus and boat traffic added its pollution to the river's rich, slightly fetid aroma, evidence of the half-hidden shacks of poor river folk, whose lives were barely less precarious than those of the local fauna. In the shallows lay the rusting wrecks of domestic appliances and automobiles; a few miles from the river lay farmsteads, villages and small towns, and beyond the city and its tidy suburbs.

To the innocent eye, when the sun beat down, the river would seem like a band of molten gold snaking through the green. The vital, restless life that teemed and squirmed beneath its surface and swarmed along its banks was momentarily hidden and the river acquired a pastoral beauty that belied a truer, darker nature.

Chapter 1

A naked woman in her early thirties came out of the house. She closed the door behind her and turned, watching the couple out near the pool. They too were naked, dancing belly to belly and cheek to cheek. The portable tape player was too loud now. All the neighbours were in bed. She stooped and turned down the volume, balancing a tray with four fresh drinks carefully on her tanned thighs. The eight-foot-high concrete fence around the back yard kept out prying eyes from the Porter patio, but the sound of sweet music from back in the big band days could antagonise their new neighbours. She didn't want that. The high fence had set tongues wagging and acted as a barrier down here in the Deep South. Delton, Georgia, the Heart of Dixie. She chuckled at the lack of Southern hospitality they'd received. The only thing warm about Georgia was the weather.

It was the middle of summer, almost midnight on a Saturday night. The air was still. Leaves hung limply in the big elm by the side of the patio. Crickets chirped softly in the thick grass beyond. A few lightning bugs flashed as they flew silently across the yard. Maria stood up, congratulating herself for spraying the insect repellent about the patio before their across-the-street neighbours and only local friends, the young Nielsens, had arrived for the back yard barbecue. All four of them had been nude for well over an hour, and not one had suffered even a hint of a mosquito bite. She made a mental note to get several cans of the spray as she walked quietly to the glider where Danny Nielsen sat transfixed, his eyes glued to the dancing couple. The girl swaying her stomach against the man's hairy abdomen was Helen, his innocent bride of less than a year.

His face retaining its sullen expression, Danny accepted the drink from Maria with a grunt. He had been against swimming in the nude from the first. He was still against it. He'd been afraid it would lead to something like this. Now that it had, he was sorry he'd let the Porters talk them into it. Helen thought it was daring, thrilling. But what did she know? She was only eighteen and had never been outside the state. He'd known better, being a man of twenty-three and not long out of the Navy. Why had he finally agreed to the nude swim?

The drinks, he decided. And the calm way both Maria and Roderick Porter had kept bringing the conversation back to how healthy nudism was. Maybe nude swimming is healthy, he thought, but things can fast get out of hand when the drinks come continuously and nobody bothers to count.

The glider jerked as Maria sat down beside him. Ice cubes tinkled as she sipped at her drink. She sighed and set her glass on the patio table. She got two cigarettes and lit them both, handing one to Danny as she leaned back and ran her soft hand lightly over his thigh.

"Thanks," Danny said. He pulled deeply on his smoke, then exhaled forcefully, his eyes never leaving the dancing couple.

"Ten minutes," Maria said in a hoarse whisper.

"What?"

She smiled, letting her cool fingers walk up the inside of his thigh. "From the looks of things, it'll only take about ten more minutes."

Danny squirmed uneasily as her fingertips neared his dick. He knew now was the time to stop her, but he said nothing. Her touch was delicate and pleasant to his alcohol-muddled mind. "What are you talking about? Ten minutes for what?"

"For sex," she said, then laughed softly as his chin dropped. "Your wife is coming on strong. Look at her."

He watched Rod's hand cup his wife's nude buttock and pull her pelvis tighter against his. He saw the hardened head of Rod's big cock poke through her white thighs. They stopped dancing. He heard Helen whimper and saw her clench her legs together, squeeze the pole of flesh between them. Rod's other hand found her neglected buttock and grasped eagerly. He moved her slowly back and forth, letting her cunt slide over the top of his shaft.

"No... No, you mustn't do that." Helen didn't sound at all convincing. She made a weak effort to pull away, then moaned as Rod jerked her roughly back against him and brought his mouth down on hers. She stood limply, accepting the kiss as Rod's hands kneaded her ass and rocked her over his stiff prick. Then, her arms suddenly going around his hairy torso, her fingers gripping harshly into his shoulders, she groaned into the quiet night air and opened her mouth to suck in his tongue.

Maria's mouth came close to Danny's ear. Her warm breath teased it, then the tip of her pink tongue darted inside his ear and licked as her hand cupped under his balls.

"Don't," Danny weakly protested, pushing her hand away as he jerked his head free of her lips and tongue. He turned and looked angrily into her eyes. "What the hell's going on here?"

"Our little party is about to come to a climax, darling," Maria answered. She licked her lips and chuckled mirthfully, her hand coming back between his legs. "Look at them," she breathed excitedly, her fingers, still cool from holding her drink, encircling his stiff and throbbing shaft.

Ignoring Maria's expert fondling of his genitals, Danny swung his head round in time to see his wife being picked up and carried over to a chaise lounge. Rod leaned over and deposited Helen on her back, then pushed her thighs apart with his hands as he came down on top of her. He pressed his mouth to hers, silencing her half-hearted protests as he positioned himself between her legs. His ass wiggled, bringing the big circumcised head of his cock to the moist and parted lips of Helen's pussy. Rod's buttocks tensed. He pushed forward slowly, stretching Helen's lips taut as they opened to accept his purplish glans between them.

Helen threw back her head, breaking the kiss as she harshly sucked in her breath. Her legs opened wider, her hips moving to make penetration easier. Arms dangling limply on either side of the chaise, eyes clenched tightly shut, Helen shuddered as Rod's big cock inched up into her vagina, stretching it, filling her cunt as it had never been filled before. Hairy balls nestled gently into the crack of her ass. She sighed, bringing her arms lazily up and clasping Rod's coarse chest tightly to her. Curly hair chafed her hardened nipples as her breasts flattened out against him. She whimpered, her legs folding over Rod's as her hands moved down to cup his muscular buttocks and pull him deeper into her, tighter against her.

The head of his dick bumped her cervix. "Ooooh! Oh shit!" She sobbed brokenly, then whimpered again and again as her hips rocked the mouth of her womb back and forth over his swollen glans.

His mouth hanging open in disbelief, Danny sat stunned as he saw his wife begin thrusting up her pelvis to meet Rod's first strokes. "Goddamn 'em," he muttered under his breath. Then in a slightly louder voice he threatened, "I'll kill him... both of them!"

Maria grinned in silence. She had heard such outbursts before. Danny would do nothing of the sort, and she knew it full well. He had sat quietly, watching for over a half-hour as Rod seduced his young wife little by little. His words were only to save face, a front to cover the sexual thrill he felt at seeing his bride accept another man in intercourse. Rod had said it would turn out this way. As always, he'd been right. Maria had a handful of throbbing cock to prove that Danny thrilled at what he saw. Rod had sized up the Nielsens the first evening they'd spent together. He'd been on the make for Helen ever since, and Danny was not exactly unappealing to Maria. In fact, the stiffened organ in her grasping hand caused her mouth to water. She dropped to her knees in front of Danny and took the cigarette butt from his hand. Pitching it into the grass, she worked her shoulders between his legs and bent her head to his groin. She skinned back his foreskin and, holding his shaft tightly, lowered her face. The entire head of his cock was covered with the clear fluid his aroused organs had produced. Her lips formed over his glans, her tongue licking at its weeping eye as he pushed weakly and ineffectively to break the contact.

"Let me suck you," she whispered seductively, then flashed out with her tongue and licked around and around his velvet crown. He groaned and released her head. "Forget Helen and Rod. Close your eyes and lean back. Relax. I want you to enjoy this as much as I'm going to."

"But they're fucking! Your husband and my wife!"

"So? It happens all the time in our social circle. Don't tell me this is the first time for you and Helen." Maria knew that it was the first extra-marital adventure for Danny and Helen. They were exactly the kind of inexperienced young marrieds that she and Rod sought out. It gave them both an added thrill to break in a new couple to mate swapping, especially when they were as innocent and unsuspecting as Danny and Helen were. She'd spoken the same lines to many horrified young husbands who'd sat trembling with excitement as their wives got their first taste of Rod's cunt-stretcher. Her words were chosen with a purpose – to put the confused husband on the defensive. No man liked to admit that he was a bumpkin, that he was unsophisticated. "Besides, what good would it do to stop them now? I think they're both enjoying it thoroughly. Let's you and I even up the score."

Somehow it all didn't seem right to Danny. He stared over at Helen, hoping that it was all a dream, that she really wasn't giving herself to Rod. What he saw inflamed him all the more. Helen, who had been a shy virgin when they married and had not once looked at another man, was giving her all to Rod. She was responding to his brutal thrusts with lustful abandon, meeting him halfway in mid-air and grunting like a sow in rut each time her ass was driven forcefully back down onto the chaise. The lewd sounds of flesh slapping on flesh caught in his ears, joining his wife's moans of pleasure and Rod's grunting encouragement that spurred her on. Helen's legs shot up and clamped around Rod's buttocks. She wailed mournfully as her tilted pelvis allowed his prick to fill her completely. Her heels beat rapidly into the cheeks of his pistoning ass, keeping time with his driving thrusts.

"Oh, Rod! Oh God, daddy... oh, sweet man!" Helen's voice was raspy with lust, her words more gruntings than words.

Rod slammed down into her, holding his cock in to the hilt and harshly grinding their pubic mounds together. He rotated his ass, rolling and stretching her cunt with the full length of his nine-inch rod. Helen's face screwed up in agonised sex pain. Her lips drew back and she bared her teeth. Her hands tightened into fists and she beat at his back. She tried to speak but only incoherent mumblings escaped her throat.

"Is it good, baby?"

"Mmmmm!"

Laughing, Rod throbbed his glans deep within her. He felt her tense, heard her sigh, then gasped himself as her strong vagina tightened down along his thick shaft.

"Again!" she shouted, her fingernails raking down his back and digging into the cheeks of his ass. "Do that again!"

"You mean this?" he asked, throbbing the head of his dick against her cervix.

"Uhgh! Yes... yes! Don't stop... more. Do it some more."

They fell into a rhythm, Rod throbbing his cock over and over and Helen answering each time by clamping the walls of her vagina tightly around him. She frantically held him to her, her fingernails leaving red welts as she clawed at his ass to keep him from pulling out even a fraction of an inch. She began to sob brokenly, tears rolling down her cheeks as the muscles of her abdomen rippled again and again.

"Oh! Oh Jesus, that's good!" Helen breathed hoarsely.

"You like that, do you?"

"Yes... shit yes! Make me come that way, Rod... make me come!"

"Already?"

"Yeah... yeah, I'm almost there!" she panted. Her eyes screwed shut and her cunt speeded up, clasping down around his cock and urging him to throb his glans more rapidly.

"God, you're a hot little bitch! Okay, baby, let loose and fly, but ease up on me. That pussy of yours is like melted butter. If you're not careful, you'll milk the juice right up from my nuts, and I'm not ready for that yet."

"Hurry... push me, daddy! Ohh... push me over!"

Gritting his teeth, Rod throbbed his cock faster and faster. Little mewling sounds came up out of her throat. Sweat popped out on her forehead and belly. Suddenly Helen stiffened. Her eyes rolled back in their sockets and her tongue licked rapidly at her parted lips. Her cunt began its fluttering dance of orgasm. Helen threw back her head and screamed out shrilly into the night, her asshole joining in and gulping at the cool air as total climax claimed her.

She fell back limply when it was over, her entire body twitching from head to toe, her lungs gasping for air. Her arms and legs fell free of Rod, her knuckles thumping against the concrete patio, the soles of her bare feet making two separate and distinct little slaps as they hit also. Her head rolled from side to side, trailing the soft, glistening tresses of her long brown hair. She whimpered softly, taking a long time to come down from the blissful heights.

Rod raised himself with stiff arms up, looming above her and grinning down into her completely relaxed face. Finally her eyes opened and she smiled up at him. He throbbed his cock and chuckled as she groaned. "That looked like a good one," he said.

"You mean there's more?"

"Shit, baby, we're just getting started. That was only the warm-up."

"I don't know if I can take any more tonight."

"Bullshit. It's time you learned what real fucking is all about. Let's show that husband of yours what you were made for."

A cold chill swept over Helen's body. With all the drinks and Rod's expert attentions, she'd forgotten all about Danny, had been carried along into a world where only she and Rod existed, where nothing mattered but physical pleasure. She jerked her head and looked toward him. His eyes glared back at her. He'd seen it all. What must he think of her now? Oh, dear God! But wait! It wasn't anger she saw in his eyes. It was lust! Danny had sat right there and watched it all. How could he have allowed it to happen? Why hadn't he stopped Rod before it was too late?

As her gaze dropped from his flushed face, Helen saw why her husband had made no move to prevent her seduction. Maria was on her knees between his widespread legs, her hair swaying jerkily as her head bobbed up and down at Danny's loins. My God! She had his dick in her mouth! She was sucking him! And to make matters worse, Danny was thoroughly enjoying the perverted act! A sense of anger and self-righteousness swept over Helen. How could Maria be so nasty? How could Danny let Maria do that animal thing to him? At least what she and Rod had done was normal. The thought assuaged her guilty conscience. Rod's thick cock stroking slowly in and out of her still sensitive pussy helped too. Piss on Danny, she thought hazily. Rod was making her feel like her own husband never had. It was good... so good! If Danny wasn't man enough to make him quit, then let him watch. Helen brought her mouth to Rod's and kissed him wetly. Wantonly, she arched her back and began hunching to increase the pleasure his hard organ afforded. She rubbed her open palms sensually up and down his back a few times, then eagerly grasped at his ass and pulled to help him hit harder into her.

Danny licked absently at his dry, parted lips. The sound of Helen's breath sucking in harshly as Rod's glans hit into her cervix once more rang obscenely in his ears. His heart was beating rapidly, violently. The sound of its "thump, thump, thump," joined the lewd slaps of Rod's hairy abdomen as he hunched into Helen again and again. His wife's throaty moans and groans added to his distress and made his head feel light and dizzy.

Again Danny's conscience stabbed unmercifully at his heart. He groaned aloud at the pain in his chest. He struggled for breath, fought for the courage to shove Maria away and go over to the chaise and pull Rod from between his young wife's legs. It was wrong – all of it! Helen shouldn't be letting him screw her! And he shouldn't be letting Maria suck so deliciously on his excited organ! He should stop it, should jerk Rod from his wife and drag her home to beat the hell out of her. Now! Do it now, his conscience screamed. Hurry, before it's too late!

Mustering all the willpower at his command, Danny shoved roughly at Maria's forehead. The wet smack of broken suction filled his ears as Maria toppled backward. Ignoring her angry outburst, he jumped to his feet and ran across the patio. The night air felt cold on his saliva-wet prick as it swayed, still hard as a rock, to and fro. His bare feet slapped the concrete. His cock slapped too, hitting wetly from one side of his stomach to the other as he ran the few steps to where Rod and Helen lay on the chaise. He stopped beside them, hesitating, unsure as to how to go about untangling the adulterous union.

Helen was moaning steadily now, her lovely face all distorted with raging lust as her head rolled from side to side. Her eyes opened and looked up at him, then closed dreamily again as if she hadn't even seen him standing above her and her big-dicked lover. Her arms were locked around Rod's muscled back, holding him tightly to her.

"Harder! Fuck harder!"

It was a command, a hungry order. The hissing words had come from Helen's mouth but the voice was not hers. Danny's mouth dropped open in disbelief. He stared dumbfounded as Helen clawed viciously at Rod's back with her long, painted nails. Her feet dropped from the chaise and hit the patio. Her heels came up off the concrete as she braced with the balls of her feet and slammed her cunt up abandonedly to Rod. Her toes curled down against the concrete and turned white from the intensity of her efforts. The muscles of her calves and thighs stood out from the strain. Her legs were spread wide, the tendons standing out like taut cords behind her flexed knees. The soft flesh of her thighs swayed with each frantic thrust of her pelvis. Just below the wet, hairy mound of her cunt the tendons on the inner slopes of her creamy white thighs stood out boldly from the soft flesh, jerking and dancing like bowstrings being rapidly plucked.

Orgasm was drawing near for them both. For a crazy second Danny considered letting them go on with the wild, jerky union. He was even more caught up in their lust now than he had been at the start. He hadn't believed it then, and thought that his eyes were playing tricks on him as Rod's huge cock spread Helen's small cunt to the very limit and inched up into her slowly until his wrinkled scrotum nestled snugly into the warm crack of her innocent young ass. But there was no doubt in his mind now. Helen had more meat in her tunnel than he, himself, would ever be able to give her. And she loved it! Goddamn her! She loved it! She was going out of her head with lust and chanting vile obscenities into Rod's ear as she clawed his back and threw her pussy up to gobble his donkey-like cock again and again.

A hoarse, unintelligible curse burst from his throat. He grabbed Helen's wrists and flung her arms to the sides, away from Rod's red-streaked back.

Helen looked up glassily at him. Saliva trickled down her cheek. Her lips were puffy and trembling. Sweat beaded her forehead and she licked wildly at her teeth and lips. Her eyes screwed shut. Her lips pulled back and bared her teeth. Her arms shot up and clasped Rod harshly to her again. "Oooh! Ouuu!" she groaned mournfully as the first waves of deep orgasm swept throughout her body. "I'm coming! Oh Rod! Darling man! Come with me... hurry... shoot it... shoot it... shoor it!"

The urgent pleas caused Rod to plunge into the dark, sweet lake of orgasmic waters right along with her. A guttural sound ripped from his throat. The cheeks of his ass dimpled as he ground his pelvis roughly into Helen's, holding the full length of his twitching cock inside her fluttering vagina. His mouth sought hers, found it and closed over her lips. His tongue shot into her mouth. He moaned a muffled moan into her oral cavity as her cheeks hollowed in suction and drew his pink spear out to the limit.

Grabbing a mass of Rod's hair, Danny jerked his head back. The sound of the broken kiss was a loud, wet slurp. Warmth covered Danny's backside. A small hand came around him and grasped harshly at his hard dick. Another small hand came around his other side and fingers enclosed his balls. The fingers squeezed down just enough to cause spears of pain to shoot up through his loins.

"Leave 'em alone, Danny. It's too late to stop them now." Maria's voice was soft, but it was more of an order than a request. Her tone held a threat.

"No! Goddamn it! No!" Danny shouted. He jerked Rod's head back roughly, enjoying the painful wail that escaped the older man's tightly stretched throat.

"Stop it!"

Maria's voice cut like a knife in his ears.

Her fingernails scraped and dug into the shaft of his cock. The sharp pain caused him to cry out and gasp, but still he tugged at Rod's head in an effort to drag the man from his wife before he went into orgasm and shot his sperm inside her heaving belly. Maria's slender fingers tightened threateningly around his balls.

"Oh-uhgg! No... no, Maria!" A dull, sickening pain swept over Danny as Maria squeezed down a little harder on his nuts.

"Turn Rod loose or I'll crush them for you!"

When Danny refused to release his grip on her husband's hair, Maria made good her promise. Smiling inwardly, secretly pleased that Danny had presented her with the opportunity to exercise her sadistic nature, Maria suddenly clamped down on his balls with all her might. Danny disappointed her. She'd hoped to hear him scream out shrilly into the night. But he didn't. Instead, he merely stiffened and heaved a choking gasp.

Releasing Rod's hair, Danny sank to his knees beside the wildly fucking couple. His hands covered his groin and he rocked back and forth, moaning and whimpering. He heard his wife sobbing out her second orgasm. It didn't matter. Nothing mattered now except the waves of nausea churning through his guts. Hands pushed at his head, forcing his face into the crack of Rod's warm and sweaty ass. The smell of shit filled his nostrils. Danny gagged. He fought against vomiting for a moment, then the smell was gone. He opened his eyes and saw a pair of hairy balls jerking rhythmically above a dancing asshole. The coarse sounds of a grunting male orgasm joined Helen's softer sighs. A trickle of come overflowed her cock-filled pussy and collected in her quivering anus.

Chapter 2

Rod left his spurting cock buried in Helen to the hilt till the spasms subsided and his balls loosened and hung limp once more. The young wife's moans had diminished to afterglow whimperings when he slowly pulled his limp and glistening organ from her vagina and stood beside the chaise. Danny was hobbling around in a circle, groaning and still holding his pain-racked nuts.

"You shouldn't have been so hard on him, baby," Rod admonished Maria. She smiled wickedly, her eyes gleaming as she watched the doubled-up young husband doing his dance of pain. Rod went to her and kissed her lips. He put his mouth to her ear and whispered, "Control yourself. Later, honey. When we get the party set up... then you can have all the fun with him you want. But not now. Be careful, or you'll scare them off."

"Her too," Maria breathed excitedly. "I've got luscious plans for Helen too."

"Tell me about it later. Let's calm them down right now or we may blow the whole bit. I'll take care of Danny. You go sit with Helen and keep her from having an attack of conscience."

Maria nodded and went to the chaise. She sat down beside Helen and smiled sweetly down into her eyes. Palming a strand of sweat-dampened hair from Helen's forehead and gently patting her abdomen at the same time, she asked, "Having a good time, little one?"

"Oh, God! I don't know what came over me. I'm sorry, Maria. I didn't mean to... I mean... Oh! Oh, I don't know how to say it."

"Hush, baby, hush. You don't have to say anything. And for God's sake don't apologise. I'm glad you and Rod made it so deliciously together."

"You're not jealous? You don't hate me?"

Maria bent and planted a motherly kiss on her forehead. "Do I act like I'm jealous? Hell no. I liked it. It gave me a thrill to see you and Rod balling. He's great, isn't he? Listen, baby, I'll loan him to you any time you want."

"Oh, Maria! Oh no, I couldn't! I just couldn't let it happen again."

"Why not? It was good, wasn't it?"

"Christ, yes! I can't deny that. Rod is really all man. He brought out nerves in me that I didn't know I had. Ohhh!"

"So? Where's the problem? Rod goes for you just as much as you go for him."

"It's wrong, Maria. So wicked!"

"Bullshit. Anything that turns you on and doesn't hurt anyone else is not wicked."

At the mention of "anyone else" Helen's head jerked up and her eyes opened wide, looking around for her husband. She spotted him out by the pool. He was glaring angrily at Rod and looked as if he might hit him at any minute. "Danny," she said softly. "It hurt Danny."

"It didn't hurt him as much as you think. It's a funny thing, Helen, but many men... how should I say it? Well, he's not as angry as he looks. Take my word for it. I've seen it a lot and his reaction is natural."

"You're wrong, Maria. He's mad, really mad. I've never seen him so mad about anything!"

Chuckling softly, Maria answered, "He's saving face, baby. That's all it amounts to, believe me."

"You think he'll get over it? You think he'll forgive me?"

"I guarantee it."

"I don't know. I don't know. Look! They're going to fight!"

Maria swung her head around in time to see Danny shove Rod backward into the swimming pool. She laughed aloud as his muscular body splashed into the water and Danny turned to stomp toward them. She got up and moved away from the chaise, giving Danny a wide berth as she walked to the pool to help Rod out. "You cooled off now, lover?" she asked, extending her hand and taking his to pull him up from the water.

Wiping the hair from his face, Rod smiled knowingly as he came out of the pool and stood dripping beside her. He took one of her nipples between his thumb and forefinger and pinched down harshly into the brown flesh.

A shiver shot through Maria's body. She whimpered. Then she pushed his hand away and hugged Rod lovingly. "Wait till they leave, darling," she whispered.

They stood by the pool, watching as Danny angrily jerked his wife to her feet and slapped her face. He went to their pile of clothes and threw Helen's dress at her, ordering her to put it on as he slid his legs into his trousers.

"What do you think?" asked Maria, her fingertips lightly teasing at Rod's lower stomach.

"I think they're made to order... putty for

the sculptor's hand to mould at will," Rod replied with a grin.

Tears streamed down Helen's cheeks as she pulled the dress over her head and wiggled into it. She reached behind her to zip it up but had to abandon the project in order to catch her shoes when Danny threw them at her one at a time. She had no time to put them on, for Danny jammed his bare feet into his loafers and came at her angrily with their underthings and stockings in his left hand. With his right hand he gripped her upper arm, digging his fingers into the soft flesh, and dragging her around the side of the house.

The gate opened and then slammed shut. Maria smiled up at Rod. "Danny's more of a man than I thought," she said. "Do you think he'll beat her?"

"Naw. He may slap her once or twice, but he won't hurt her. I wish we had their bedroom wired for sound. They're going to have the wildest screw they've ever had in a few minutes, and I'd like to hear it."

"Come on in to the house, sculptor. There's going to be a wild fuck taking place in our bedroom tonight, too," Maria said, her fingers eagerly enfolding Rod's re-awakening prick.

*   *   *

Heading straight for their bedroom, Danny dragged Helen through the house without a word. He pulled her cringing form through the doorway and slammed the door shut. Then he swung her roughly round and sent her sprawling on the bed. Throwing their underthings on the dresser and knocking her perfume and make-up articles off onto the floor, he hissed, "You pig! Slut! Whore! Bitch!"

Helen sat up, cringing in the middle of the bed as Danny stood glaring hatefully at her. She wanted to admit he was right. The names he called her... they were true and accurate. She couldn't blame him for the outburst and the angry accusations, for the same words had been running through her own mind. Danny had only given voice to the way she felt about her insane lapse of self-control. A fresh flood of tears obscured her vision and cascaded down her cheeks. She sobbed aloud and buried her face in her hands. "I'm sorry, Danny. I'm so sorry," she whimpered through her hands.

"Sorry? Sorry? Is that supposed to make it all right? No! Goddamn you, no! You made a fool of me, you little whore! I loved you. I thought you were a good girl. Good girl! Shit, what a fucking laugh! You're nothing but a wanton slut who had me fooled. Boy! Did you have me fooled! You know what? I even believed you were a virgin when we got married. Isn't that a laugh? How'd you do it, bitch? How'd you make the blood come the first time I fucked you? But then, thinking back on it, there wasn't much blood, was there? Just a few drops at the most... barely stained the sheet, as I recall. What'd you do? Hold your cunt lips together to make it feel so tight? Yeah... that's what you did. I remember how you put it in for me. You weren't concerned so much with putting it in nice and easy as you were with making me think it was a tight and virginal pussy, were you?"

"No, Danny. That's not true. I was a virgin... you know I was. I didn't try to fool you, honey. I've never tried to fool you about anything. Oh, God! No, you mustn't think that."

"Shut up! The blood. What'd you do to make yourself bleed? Scratch yourself with those long fingernails? Must have. Had to be that way, because as soon as I got my cock all the way in you it was like you just... opened up. Yeah! You liked it right from the start. You shouldn't have... now that I think about it. It should have hurt you the first time. Most girls don't like it for a few months. I read that in a good book. Yeah! It's an ordeal for them at first, sex is. But not you. Goddamn it! Not for you it wasn't! You hunched that pussy right up to me the very first time!"

"I loved you, Danny... that's why! I wanted it to be good for you. It did hurt me, but I didn't let on because I knew you wanted it to feel good for me too. I acted like it did for your sake, darling... that's all. I swear that's the way it was. You were the first... the only man for me."

Danny glared coldly at her. His voice was sharp and cutting as he spat, "I don't believe I was the first... not now... not after what I saw tonight. You lay right there in front of me and let that son-of-a bitch stick his mule cock in you."

Anger mounted in Helen until it overcame the humiliation of her lustful abandon on the Porters' patio. "Why, you self-righteous prick! I saw you and Maria too, you know! You pervert! She sucked your dick, and don't try to deny that you loved it! Shit yes, you liked it! You let her take it in her mouth while you watched Rod and me fuck! Why didn't you stop us if you wanted to? I'm your wife, aren't I? All you had to do was grab me by the hand and drag me home. That's all! You could have stopped it before it even got started good. Why didn't you?"

"I didn't believe my eyes... that's why. I thought, 'No. No, it can't be happening. Helen wouldn't let it. She loves me too much to give it to another guy.' Now I know better. You're a damned nympho... wouldn't surprise me if I came home some night and found you letting a black man hump you."

"Danny! That's enough now!" Helen jumped up and slapped Danny resoundingly, her fingers leaving red splotches on his pink cheek.

Instinctively Danny reacted by returning her slap. In his frustrated anger he hit her harder than he meant to, and sent her sprawling on her back across the bed once more. Then, grunting like an animal, he bent over her and grabbed at the collar of her dress. One frantic jerk ripped the dress down to her waist. Her bare breasts jiggled as the bed rolled and jerked. Before he realised what he was doing, Danny heard his wife screaming and pleading with him to stop. He saw what he was doing too late to stop the last blow, and his open palm hit into her soft breast again. The loud slapping noise echoed inside his head and joined her moan of pain.

He was hurting her. Under normal circumstances Danny would have been horrified by his actions, but this was not a normal situation. The sounds of her anguish only incited him to further brutality. He took both her nipples between his thumbs and forefingers. Grinning down at her, he began tightening his hold, watching the astonishment in her lovely face as his fingertips bit deeper and deeper into her brown areolae.

Sharp spears of pain shot out from her breasts, making her whimper all the more. "Don't Danny! Please stop. You're hurting me, honey. Ohh, you're hurting me."

Sneering down at her pain-racked face, Danny pinched all the harder. "I ought to kill you!" he shouted, his fingertips biting brutally into her nipples and twisting at the same time.

"Aargh! aargh! God... oh God! Hurts... oh, it hurts!" Helen moaned pitifully. She writhed in agony, but though her hands were free she made no effort to escape. Instead she bore the sharp pain with gasps and groans as Danny twisted her tender flesh this way and that. She sucked in her breath harshly as he pulled out her nipples and tried to tear them from her body. To her utter amazement, Helen found herself reaching out for Danny's dick, her fingers clawing frenziedly at his fly in an effort to get it open.

The intense pain had changed somehow. It still hurt terribly, but there was something else now added to it. It hurt good! It hurt deliciously good! She jerked open Danny's fly and grasped his hard cock, pulling it from his pants and eagerly working her hand up and down its pulsating shaft.

"You cock-hungry bitch!" Danny hissed,

staring down at her with an obvious mixture of hatred and lust showing in his face.

"Danny! Oh God, honey... fuck me!!"

"What's the matter? Didn't Porter give you enough cock for one night?"

"To hell with Rod... to hell with everybody. I want you, Danny... you! I love you, darling... love you so much, so much!"

A grin spread over Danny's face as he stood up and undid his pants. After letting his pants fall to the floor and kicking them off to the side, he bent over Helen again and ripped the dress completely open. Palming his stiff organ, Danny slapped it several times up against his belly, letting it sway as it fell each time. He watched Helen's eyes, saw her licking her lips and heard her panting lust as she stared at his dancing penis.

She spread her legs and held out her arms. "Give it to me. Now... give it to me now! Don't tease me any more, darling. I'm on fire for you... come to me... fuck me!"

Coming on top of her, Danny positioned himself between her legs. He brought the head of his organ to her hot, moist cunt and ran it up and down the length of her twitching cleft.

"Put it in, honey. Oh God, put it in me before I go out of my mind!"

"You like my cock, huh?" Danny asked, teasing her verbally as he stroked up her pussy again with the head of his cock.

"Yes... oh yes! I love your cock, darling... love it... love it!"

She tried to reach for his organ and help get it into her vagina, but Danny slapped her hand away. "Not yet!" he said imperiously. "There's something you've got to do first."

With that, he pulled away from her pelvis and crawled straddle-legged up her body, stopping with his cock in her face as he sat unconcernedly down on her chest and soft breasts.

"Danny? Darling, what in the world?"

"Kiss it!"

"No, Danny! Don't make me do that. That's perversion!"

"I didn't ask you for a damned lecture. Kiss it!"

"No, honey... please, no. It'll make me feel like a whore."

"You are a whore," Danny retorted quickly.

Helen shook her head in protest. She meant to tell Danny that he was wrong. However, she had no chance for words, for both her husband's hands grabbed into her hair and jerked her face toward his genitals. She had no choice but to allow her lips to be drawn to his glans, there to be moved slowly from side to side as he rocked her head painfully back and forth.

"Kiss it," he ordered, holding her head still

at last, with the weeping eye of his cock part way between her soft lips.

Whimpering at the pain in her scalp, her mind reeling at the unspeakable indignity being forced on her by her own husband, Helen timidly pursed her lips and smacked a weak kiss around the tip of his glans. "Again," she heard him bark. As her lips pursed for the second time, she felt his cock slip through them and poke at her teeth. His musky-tasting glans pressed harder and he held her hair in his trembling hands. "Open your mouth, Helen," his voice said, as if from afar.

It was no use fighting against it. He only pulled her hair all the more and kept her lips over his glans. Finally she did as he wanted and opened her teeth to let his organ slip into her mouth. His flavour was strong on her sensitive tongue. She'd expected to feel revolted with a mouthful of male organ. All her life she'd heard how perverted and dirty it was to let a boy put his penis in your mouth. Maybe it is perverted, she thought hazily, and maybe it's dirty too. But it's something else – it's thrilling as all hell! The urge to resist further drained from her body suddenly, leaving her weak and trembling with lust. She stroked her palms up Danny's legs and cupped his ass firmly, her hands pulling him toward her, getting his cock deeper into her mouth. Deeper and deeper, until her lips felt the coarse hair of his pubic mound and the head of his rod hit into the soft membrane at the back of her throat.

"That's it, baby... suck it... suck it good!"

Danny's raspy encouragement whipped her lust to a higher peak. Her tongue licked eagerly at the big, sensitive vein along the bottom of his shaft. Her cheeks hollowed in harsh suction around his rod. Her fingernails dug excitedly into the quivering cheeks of his buttocks and held him in place as she pushed her head forward and strained for more. The fatty tissue of his pubic mound gave a little under the pressure of her wide-open teeth and swollen lips. The head of his cock jabbed into the back of her throat and tried in vain to negotiate the downward bend and fill her swallowing throat as well as her sucking mouth.

"Oh, baby... God, baby... Oh God!" Danny's eyes were wide open, staring down at the lustful expression on Helen's face. It was too erotic to bear. His balls drew up tight against his body in readiness for orgasm. His glans twitched and began a rhythmical throbbing. It was too soon... too soon. Suddenly he backed away from her and jerked his almost-out-of-control penis from her harshly sucking oral cavity.

A loud slurping noise filled the room as Helen unexpectedly lost her mouthful of blood-engorged meat. She groaned in protest and licked at her lips, her eyes coming open to stare hungrily at her husband's spit-slick prick. "Give it back, Danny! Let me suck it. I want to, darling, I want to! Let me suck it all the way... come in my mouth... Yes! Oh, do come in my mouth!"

But that was not what Danny had in mind. To force his newly unfaithful wife to take his dick in her mouth and suck on it was not meant to give her pleasure. No. He'd only done it to humiliate her, to treat her like the whore she'd proved herself that very night to be. It had surprised him as much as Helen when suddenly it was no longer a game of put-down, but turned instead to a lewd new pleasure for them both. "Pig!" he shouted, as much in anger at himself for enjoying it as a verbal slap at his violently sexed-up wife. He slapped her viciously across the face and recoiled when her moan of pleasure rather than pain fell on his ears.

His mind reeling in frustration, Danny got up and stood beside the bed. Helen moaned mournfully and held out her arms to him. Her legs opened invitingly. Her pelvis heaved with urgent desire, raising her smooth buttocks up off the mattress and moving in little hunching, circular motions.

"Fuck me... Please, darling, I need you... I need you..."

The hair surrounding her cunt was wet with sweat and sex juices, plastered to her skin in tight little curls. Her outer lips were standing wide open, blood engorged and swollen with raw lust. Her inner lips also protruded outward, and were coloured a fiery red in testimony to her agitated state of sexual need. Resembling a small penis in full erection, her clitoris had left the protection of its hood and stood out boldly at the top of her elliptical opening.

The sight was even more frustrating to Danny. He stood gawking down at the wild woman his wife had become. His penis throbbed eagerly as his eyes took in the condition of Helen's cock-hungry pussy. He had never seen it in quite this condition. And there was something else he saw, something that both thrilled and repelled him. The something else was not a natural part of Helen's sexual excitement, nor of any other female, for that matter. It was white and sticky-looking. The inch of skin between her cunt and asshole was covered with it. In her asshole itself was a small pool of the white fluid that almost obscured the anus-brown colour.

"Hurry, darling, hurry," Helen murmured. She clamped down the muscles of her vagina as if caressing an imaginary penis within it. The motion sent a blob of Rod's deeply planted come rushing down her tunnel.

Unable to tear his gaze from her cunt, Danny saw the mass of his wife's adulterous lover's come slide obscenely out of her vagina. It stopped just inside her crimson-red inner lips and jiggled there momentarily, then oozed out and pooled in the wide-spread opening of her young pussy. The sight drew him like a magnet. As if hypnotised, Danny bent over his wife and brought his face closer to her steaming slit. Her inner muscles relaxed and the pool of Rod's come was slurped back up inside her belly.

With an alien groan ripping from his throat, Danny put both his hands on her lower abdomen and pressed down. The come again appeared at the end of her vagina. He pressed harder, trying to see it come out the rest of the way and lie in her open cunt-lips like it did before. It refused to leave the warm comfort of her vagina.

Helen could feel her husband's hot breath as it bathed her vulva. One hand now pressed at her stomach while the fingers of another probed through her sensitive inner lips and played maddeningly just inside the tube of her vagina. "Danny! Danny? Danny... what are you doing, honey?"

An animal-like grunt was his only answer for perhaps twenty seconds or more. Then her buttocks were hoisted up suddenly and Danny was kneeling between her legs, bringing his face up awfully close to her crotch and pushing her thighs up and wider apart.

"Honey? Danny?"

His voice was unrecognisable, a raspy exhalation of breath. "Squeeze down again... like you had a cock up you!"

Obediently she again caressed an imaginary penis and held the walls of her vagina clamped tightly together. She felt Danny tremble violently as his fingers gripped harshly into the soft flesh of her elevated thighs. She raised her head and looked down into his face. A gasp of astonishment escaped her open mouth at the sight of his tortured facial expression. His eyes were wide and glassy. His mouth hung open and saliva drooled down his chin. His lips twitched spasmodically out of control.

"Honey... No, Danny... No! Oh, no!"

But it was too late, and if he heard her protestations, Danny gave no sign of heeding her pleas. With a pitiful little whimper he dropped his face to her genitals and claimed her cunt with his mouth. Helen was dumbfounded by his action. Never had he given any inkling of a desire to kiss her there... never. Why now? She was in such a mess after Rod had finished with her.

"Oh God... Let me up, Danny. I'll go douche it out for you, honey. Then you can suck me, but not now."

Still Danny paid her no heed. His hands went under her ass and cupped her tightly to his face. His lips tightened over her cunt in harsh suction and his tongue shot up into her and licked... licked and licked and licked, until she thought she'd go out of her mind from the sheer pleasure of it.

With a last burst of decency, she pushed his face away and looked down pleadingly into his lust-glazed eyes. He gulped and smacked his puffy lips. A trickle of Rod's fluid lay in a ragged, white moustache on his upper lip. She watched, more fascinated than horrified now, as he licked it off and took it into his mouth.

Chapter 3

No one stirred in either the Porter or Nielsen houses. Both couples slept until the sun was high up in the sky. It was the usual Sunday routine for Maria and Rod Porter. Both had dropped all pretences of a religious belief while in college, many years past. Maria considered herself an agnostic; Rod never bothered to try and classify himself.

On most Sundays Danny and Helen got up in time to attend both Sunday school and church services. Not that they were devoutly religious. It was merely the easiest way to get along, since the church they normally attended was pastored by Helen's father. It was a small church, a fundamentalist sect, and Helen's father shouted his sermons from the pulpit in the best tradition of a vanishing style of hell-fire oratory that sometimes made the hair on the back of Danny's neck stand up in fright.

That Sunday Danny awoke slowly. He glanced sleepily over at the clock on the bedside table. He groaned aloud. Sunday school was over and the church service was more than ten minutes underway. There'd be hell to pay at supper. Though Helen's mother was a wonderful cook, no one would enjoy the meal. Her father would see to that, as he always did when they failed to show up for Sunday morning worship. A private sermon was in order, and though he'd heard it enough times to memorise it word for word, it still left him feeling like the worst of sinners for not caring sufficiently for Helen to look after her soul by making sure that she was in a front pew when her father delivered his message of the week to the small flock.

Reaching for a cigarette, Danny wondered why they'd forgotten to set the alarm. He had the cigarette in his mouth and lit before he was awake enough to remember anything of last night's activities. His hand trembling slightly, he shook out the match and sucked a deep pull of smoke down into his lungs. The dead match fell into the ashtray with a tiny tinkle. He exhaled with a sigh, turning to look at Helen.

A sleeping angel. That's what she reminded him of. Her appearance this morning was no different than on any other morning. The features of her lovely face were calm and serene. A radiant innocence seemed to emanate from her.

Could it have been a dream? Grotesque mental images of his pure wife lost in lustful abandon with Rod Porter careened across Danny's mind. It had seemed so real, so painful. Had he only dreamt it? But wait – what about the shameful way he and Helen had clawed at each other after they got home?

Danny ran one hand under himself and felt his back. He winced in pain at the swollen welts left by Helen's long fingernails. The final climax of their private orgy had brought out a purely animal part of his wife that Danny had never before suspected. She'd clawed viciously at his back and yelled at the top of her lungs for him to come with her. After he had, they'd rolled apart and fell immediately into a deep sleep.

Some time during the night Helen had managed to pull the cover up over her nude body. Danny now eased it back gently. The sight of her full breasts rising and falling in the rhythm of sleep brought a stifled gasp. They were covered with bruises where his fingers had slapped so roughly.

No. It was not a dream. Helen was no longer the innocent young bride. She was now an adulteress, having taken her lover right in front of her own husband's eyes.

That was bad enough. The full knowledge of the situation made Danny cringe. Helen's whore-like action was unthinkable, almost unbelievable. Recalling how his wife so passionately responded to Rod made Danny's cheeks flush in anger.

But there was something else, something that was much worse, to Danny's way of thinking. He'd felt it last night, while he sat watching Rod insert his big cock into Helen. The sight had brought out two emotions from the very depths of his being. The two emotions had fought with each other, had held him seated and helpless as Rod took his place between Helen's opened legs.

The lewd mental picture of Rod's big dick entering Helen's sweet pussy passed now before his eyes. It called forth the same two emotions, and once again he was trembling excitedly. Almost in one swift leap his prick jerked up stiff and throbbing. Danny took it in his hand and squeezed. He closed his eyes.

Once again Helen writhed ecstatically under Rod. Her whimpering moans of fulfillment echoed inside Danny's head. Hairy nuts jerked spasmodically above a dancing female asshole. A young pussy completely filled with a huge, spurting cock could not contain the massive load of sperm being shot forcefully into its depths. Sperm, white and slick, oozed out around the tautly stretched cunt-lips and trickled into a pool in Helen's anus. Danny groaned as he felt a wave of pleasure pass through his loins. Gritting his teeth at the intense orgasm, he let the come squirt from his tightly-held organ and fall in warm, wet jets onto his naked stomach.

Shamefacedly, Danny rose and went into the bathroom for his shower.

Helen had not moved when he came out several minutes later. He stood over her, looking down into her sleeping face as he tied the sash of his robe. Wincing again at the bruises on her lovely breasts, Danny pulled the covers back up to her shoulders. After kissing her tenderly on the forehead, Danny went to get the paper from the yard.

In the kitchen he put on the coffee, then sat down to read the paper while it percolated. He intended to prepare breakfast and serve it to Helen in bed. It was the least he could do after mistreating her so badly last night. She was no more to blame for what had happened at the Porters' than he was. He resolved never to throw it in her face. He would not even mention it, he decided.

Helen awoke to find Danny already out of bed. She looked at the clock and found that it was nearly noon. They'd missed both Sunday school and church. She groaned. Now she would experience the anger of two men, her husband's for what had happened the previous night and her father's for missing services.

Reluctant to get up and face the day ahead, Helen lay back in bed. She was trying to figure out what kind of defence would be best when Danny confronted her, when she heard his footsteps coming toward the bedroom. As yet unprepared for the attack she knew was coming, Helen closed her eyes and feigned sleep. To her astonishment, the attack never came. Instead, Danny bent lovingly over her and kissed her lightly on the nose, then tiptoed from the room without saying a word.

"Danny?" Her puzzled voice stopped him in the bedroom doorway. She studied his face. There was no anger or hatred in his expression. He was smiling embarrassedly at her, like a small boy caught with his hand in the cookie jar. "Why didn't you wake me up, honey?"

"Ah, I forgot to set the alarm. When I woke up it was already too late for church."

If he's not going to mention it, I'm certainly not, Helen decided. She forced a weak smile. "You must be starved. Want me to fix breakfast now?"

"No!" he said hurriedly. "No. You just stay right there. I've got coffee ready and bacon in the pan. I'll make breakfast and bring it in here to you. Want some coffee now?"

Helen's eyes popped wide open. She couldn't believe her ears but dared not ask him to repeat it. She nodded her head and mumbled that that would be very nice, very thoughtful of him, then watched him smile broadly and hurry off to the kitchen.

Breathing a sigh of relief, she lay back and pondered the craziness of the situation. She could hear him out in the kitchen, opening and closing the refrigerator, rattling a coffee cup.

A moment later he came walking carefully into the bedroom, a cup of steaming coffee clattering softly on the saucer in his hand. Smiling nervously, he approached the bed and cleared a place on the night-stand to put the coffee. He straightened and stood beside the bed, pushing her ruined dress under it with his foot.

"Thank you, darling," Helen murmured as she sat up and reached for the coffee. She sipped at it, looking up into his eyes and trying to smile as if nothing was wrong. But her smile was weak, unconvincing.

"Hope I didn't get too much cream in it for you," Danny said.

"No." Helen returned quickly. "It's fine... just the way I like it." She took another sip, as if to prove that it pleased her. When she looked back up, she saw Danny staring at her breasts. She looked down at them and saw the bruises for the first time. Automatically she gasped and reached up to touch the livid splotches.

A pained expression swept over Danny's face. He took the cup from her hand and put it back on the night-stand, then knelt quickly beside the bed and began kissing the ugly streaks on her breasts. "I'm sorry I hurt you."

Helen stroked her fingers through his hair, letting him go on with his soothing kisses until he began to sob. The sound of her husband crying confused her all the more. She took his head between her hands and pushed him away. Tears formed in her own eyes as she searched his pain-racked face. "It's all right, honey. I had it coming... oh God, Danny! We've got to talk about it, honey. Last night... it was all so crazy and mixed up. I don't know what came over me... or you. What happened to us, Danny? Why did we act that way?"

"I don't want to talk about it, Helen. It's in the past. Ignore it. Forget the past."

"Oh, Danny... that won't help. We can't just ignore it. That won't make it go away, darling.

I'm ashamed of how I acted. Let's talk about it honey. I need to. Maybe if we could talk it out and understand why we did it, maybe that would help us get over it."

"Just forget it, darling. I forgive you for what happened at the Porters. Can you forgive me for what happened after?"

"Oh yes, Danny... yes, darling. I forgive you," she moaned, hugging his face once again to her sore breasts. "I forgive you. It isn't that. It's me. I feel so ashamed for what I did. So ashamed... and I don't even understand why. I don't love Rod. You're the only man I love. I don't understand what came over me. I can't forgive myself. I feel so cheap... so guilty. I betrayed you, Danny."

Danny drew away from her and held her shoulders. "Look, Helen," he said softly. "It's best to just forget about it... to go on living and act like it never happened. I don't want to think about it any more... okay?"

Though reluctant to drop the matter without some answer which would partly assuage her guilty conscience, Helen nodded her head. "All right, Danny. If that's the way you want it. Shall I fix breakfast now?"

A certain smile of triumph and satisfaction always came over Danny's face when he watched a customer sign a new, sizable insurance policy. He could not explain his feelings at those times. It was a subconscious feeling, a knowledge that things were going the way he wanted them to, that he would benefit in the future as well as at the moment of the sale. He smiled that same smile now, at Helen.

Partly drawing Helen to him and partly bending toward her, he kissed her lips firmly but tenderly, as if sealing a bargain. "No, sweet baby. I'll fix breakfast for you. I want to. Now you just relax and drink your coffee. How many eggs do you want?"

"Just one," she said contentedly. "Over easy." Then she lay back and watched Danny leave for the kitchen again. She sipped at the coffee.

It was nice. Danny was right to insist they forget about it. She felt an extra warmth in her breast at the sound of cracking eggshells, an almost overflowing of love for Danny.

But something puzzled her, didn't seem to fit. Danny's smile. It was such a strange smile, such a knowing smile. He'd never smiled at her quite like that before, yet she had seen it. That first night she met him. He'd smiled exactly that way when her father signed the papers of the insurance policy Danny had come to sell him. Could that mean anything, she wondered?

Reproaching herself for being so suspicious, for wanting to analyse everything until it made sense, she took another swallow of coffee. The coffee seemed to stick in her throat and form a lump. Some of the warm liquid went down her windpipe, causing her to cough and splutter. That it might be a bad omen flashed across her mind. She shook her head and laughed. That's silly, she thought. But still it bothered her.

What had Maria said about Danny last night? She couldn't recall the older woman's words. The words were not so important anyway. It was the way Maria had said it. Helen had felt that Maria was in reality telling her much more than her few words had conveyed.

"Quit it, Helen!" she said aloud to herself. "Cud chewing is for cows, not people."

*　　*　　*

Monday morning. A beautiful day. The radio blared triumphantly in the laundry room. Helen hummed happily along with the voice coming from the radio. She pulled a load of freshly washed clothes from the washer. In time to the beat of the music, she dropped the still steaming clothes into a plastic basket. At last her probing hand found nothing. She peered down into the washer and saw one of Danny's socks sticking to the side. Pulling it loose, she stepped over to the last load of dirty clothes. She rolled the damp sock between her hands until it was a warm ball, then pitched it basketball-fashion on top of the clean clothes in the basket.

"You're the one I've been looking for," she accused, bending over to scoop up a double armload of the final pile of washing.

She dropped the last load into the washer, retrieved the three pieces still on the floor, basketballed them into the washer aswell and set the dials on the machine. She added detergent and stood watching until the machine seemed capable of finishing without her.

Hoisting the basket of wet clothes to her hip, Helen went out of the back door and across the yard to the already partly full clothes line at the rear of their lot. Still singing gaily, she hung the clothes out one piece at a time to dry under the hot Georgia sun.

The world was a wonderful place to live. Helen felt it in every nerve of her being. Danny had been so considerate of her, so loving and tender. Like a queen – that's how he'd made her feel. Breakfast in bed, then taking her part when Dad gave her a bad time at supper. And last night – wow! The way Danny had made love to her so passionately, so long and drawn out! On the couch in the den, ignoring his favourite TV programmes and bringing her to orgasm after orgasm before he would allow himself any pleasure at all.

Lazing about in love's afterglow, they had never felt closer.

It was the same this morning. She'd made breakfast and it was eaten at the table, but the closeness was still between them, the feeling of oneness, of fusion one with the other. It was like their honeymoon all over again, only better. The memory of Rod and Saturday night was like a long-ago nightmare, pushed so far back in her mind that it had a feeling of unreality about it. It was as though it had never actually happened.

Helen was hanging out the last piece of wash when she felt eyes on her back. She put the last clothes-peg in place before turning toward the woman opening her gate. It was Maria. A sense of apprehension flooded over Helen. She didn't want to see Maria, wouldn't know what to say to her under the circumstances. For an uncomfortable moment she considered fleeing out of the back gate and running down the alley.

Then it was too late. Maria called a friendly hello and waved as she came toward her. Hesitantly Helen returned the smile. She picked up her empty basket and went toward the house. They met midway in the backyard. Embarrassedly, Helen invited Maria in for coffee.

Not a word about Saturday night. Maria

rattled on and on about one thing after another, never once mentioning the degrading scene that ended the patio barbecue. It was disarming to Helen. Maria acted so natural, so friendly, as if nothing at all had happened.

When the coffee cups became empty, Maria took them over to the pot and refilled them, chatting all the while about the week-long mission that Rod and his flight crew had left on from the Air Force base that morning. Maria admitted that she envied Rod and his career. It wasn't that she minded him being away from home when he had to fly. Not at all. She was jealous, she confided. Secretly she longed to be a pilot, a colonel like Rod. He got all the fun – going to so many different places, ordering about those men under him, feeling the awesome power of those monstrous jet engines and knowing that he controlled such a force completely, had it right at his fingertips.

An intense expression came over Maria's face as she talked about the power of the big bomber that Rod flew. She saw it as an extension of her husband himself, and readily admitted that she would gladly change places with him, if it were only possible.

The look in Maria's eyes unnerved Helen. She awkwardly and abruptly switched the conversation to another subject, a more feminine topic. Occasionally she thought of bringing up Saturday night. She wanted to talk about it, yet she didn't want to. Things were going so smoothly. Maria seemed not to remember it. Danny had told her to forget it, and gave every indication that he had forgotten it himself. Yet it troubled Helen. Seeing Maria had brought it back into her mind.

After a while Maria stood up and announced that she had to go out to the commissary. She invited Helen along. After Maria told her how much cheaper groceries and cigarettes were at the base, Helen gladly accepted. It was a chance to save money, and Helen prided herself on her thrifty nature. Had she known that it was illegal for a civilian to shop at a military commissary, she would not have gone. In her naïvety, however, Helen quickly changed out of her housedress and wrote a quick note for Danny in case he should come home unexpectedly for lunch, then tucked her purse under her arm and went with Maria.

The air policeman at the base gate snapped to attention when he saw Maria's red Volkswagen coming at him. He motioned the car on through the gate without stopping them, then brought his hand up in a salute as they came nearer. As he recognised Maria, he smiled broadly and winked, still holding the salute. Smiling back at the tall, handsome airman, Maria threw him a kiss as the car swept past and into the base.

"They sure are friendly," commented Helen.

"They aren't all that friendly," Maria chuckled. "That one's a doll, though."

"He is good-looking. Is he a friend of yours and Rod's?"

"Just mine. Rod doesn't know him."

"Oh."

"No, no, baby. Not like that. He teaches karate to a group of us wives one afternoon a week."

"Oh," Helen said again, relief telling in her voice this time.

Maria drove slower now that they were on the base. Finally she pulled into a parking lot and nosed the car into a slot. "Come on," she said, getting out of the car.

As soon as they were inside the building, Helen knew it couldn't be the commissary. It was dark and music was playing on a juke-box. It was a cocktail lounge!

"What's the matter, baby?"

"I shouldn't be here. Danny wouldn't like it."

"You can have a soda if you'd rather, but I can't face the commissary without a good belt," Maria chuckled. "Come on, now. Quit your worrying and let's sit down. All the girls stop here before fighting the mob."

Though Helen did notice several tables with two or three women smoking and talking as they sipped at drinks, it looked as if Maria somewhat exaggerated the point by saying that they all did. Feeling slightly wicked, and as conspicuous as a sore thumb, she followed Maria to a corner table and took a seat that permitted her a view of the room.

The waiter came over and Maria ordered a margarita. "What do you want, honey?"

"The same as you," Helen told her, surprised at her own words. She didn't even know what a margarita was. Her answer just popped out as if her tongue couldn't bother to wait until her mind decided.

The drink was good. A little salty but very tasty. Halfway down the glass Helen watched Maria fire up a smoke. She noticed a man sitting at the bar, watching them. It made Helen uneasy. He was a Negro. She mentioned it to Maria and pointed him out.

To Helen's utter amazement Maria smiled broadly and waved at the man, then motioned for him to join their table. "Thanks for telling me, honey. That's Buck. He's a pilot in Rod's squadron."

The Negro officer brought his drink and came to the table. He was so tall that Helen had to lean back her head to see his face as Maria introduced them. God, he's handsome, she thought, black or not. He wore a thin, well-trimmed moustache and had the fullest, softest-looking lips she'd ever seen. She watched the lips pull into a smile, baring the whitest of white teeth.

"Hi," he said, extending his hand toward Helen.

No "Pleased to meet you, Mrs. Nielsen," or anything like that, just a grinning "Hi". Without realising what she was doing, Helen grinned back and said, "Hi," putting her small white hand out and watching it disappear as brown skin engulfed and pumped it a couple of times. Then he was saying, "Glad to know you," and Helen had her hand back again. She watched in fascination as the brown face leaned over Maria and kissed her a friendly peck on the mouth. There was a tingling in her lips to match the one in her hand as Helen watched the man sit down directly across the table from her.

"What the hell are you doing here, Buck?" asked Maria. "Aren't you supposed to be flying the mission with the rest of the boys?"

It was as if Maria had slapped him in the face. His brilliant smile vanished instantly. A beaten, hangdog expression replaced it. "Didn't Rod tell you?"

Sensing that something was drastically wrong, Maria put her hand soothingly on top of his. "Tell me what, baby? Is anything wrong?"

"I've been permanently grounded," he said dumbly, as if he still could not believe it himself.

"Oh no!" Maria wailed. "That's terrible!"

"For me it is. A desk jockey at thirty-two. Shit! There ain't no justice," he snapped. Then he looked at Helen apologetically. "Pardon my French, please."

"It's all right, baby," Maria soothed. "It's all right. Say it again if you want to. I know how you loved flying."

He nodded.

"Can't you appeal it? I mean, are you sure it's permanent?"

He shook his head. "Flight surgeon's orders," he explained. "Reflexes aren't fast enough any more."

Maria got to her feet and held out her hand, singing down at the saddened brown face. "Dance with me. That always livens you up, and usually puts a smile on your face."

Buck forced a smile. He took her hand and got up, saying, "What about your husband, lady? Won't he be jealous?"

Maria winked at him and grinned, then put her arm around his waist and they went to the jukebox.

They bugalooed the first dance. Watching Buck go through the motions expertly and with such ease made Helen wonder how his reflexes could possibly be any better than they were. He really knew how to dance! The next song was slower, and Maria glided in close to Buck. She put her head on his shoulder and her arms about his body as if they were the only two people in the place. She brought her mouth up to his ear and whispered.

Helen wondered what was said. Buck glanced over her way and whispered back to Maria, then they came walking hand in hand back to the table.

"Up, girl," Maria ordered. "Do your patriotic duty and dance with the major."

Getting to her feet, Helen wondered if she ought to dance with him. She wanted to. Danny was such a terrible dancer, and she did love it so. Then he was smiling, taking her hand and leading her away from the table. The next thing she knew she was in his arms and they were moving about the floor. There was something about Buck, something that made her Georgia mind forget that he was black and she was white.

It felt so natural to be dancing with him. He was a good dancer, very smooth. His hand caressed the small of her back, drawing her body closer to his. Her breasts came in contact with his chest. Allowing them to flatten against him, she put her head on his shoulder and watched the brown skin of his neck and his ear.

Both his hands were on her now, below the small of her back, resting on the upper slopes of her buttocks.

A wave of dizziness swept over Helen. The drink? She giggled and let Buck pull her belly up tight against his. Then she felt it. There was nothing wrong with his reflexes in the sex department! He was getting a hard-on! She could feel it growing bigger and harder against her soft stomach. She fought back a whimper. She wanted to pull away from contact with him but could not force herself to do it!

Mercifully the music stopped and he stepped away from her, quickly taking her hand and leading her back to the table. He thanked her, told Maria he had to go, picked up his hat, and left.

Chapter 4

A sense of foreboding clutched unrelentingly at Helen's guts. Her fingers trembled as she picked up the hairbrush and stepped in front of the full-length mirror in her and Danny's bedroom. It showed in her face, too. She should be happy, smiling. They were going to a party. Instead, the face looking back at her from the mirror appeared tense and drawn.

She forced herself to smile and began brushing her hair.

The sound of spraying water stopped abruptly. Danny stepped out of the shower, still humming happily, and reached for a towel. Vigorously he began drying the water from his body. Helen shook her head in wonder. How could Danny feel that way? She hadn't wanted to accept Maria's invitation herself, and had been sure that Danny would flatly refuse to go to their party. She'd put off mentioning it to him until this morning, even though Maria had first asked them to come after they got back from the commissary on Monday.

At the time, she'd told her no. Maria hadn't argued, and simply changed the subject and went on talking. The next day she'd asked again. Again the answer was a simple no. Maria hadn't pressed it. The same thing happened on Wednesday. Helen again politely refused on Thursday. This time Maria wanted to know why. Helen told her.

"Danny won't come," she'd said unwillingly, sure that Maria would want to discuss the sordid details that she herself would sooner leave unspoken. But Maria had merely smiled knowingly as she got out a cigarette and lit it. Then she exhaled thoughtfully and looked her right in the eye. "How do you know until you ask him, Helen?"

It was up to Helen then. She could either explain her reasoning to Maria, that Danny would never consent to a continued friendship with Rod after what had happened, or she could save herself the embarrassment of such a personal conversation and tell Maria that she would ask Danny. She agreed to ask Danny if he wanted to attend the party.

Working up the courage to ask him was a difficult thing for Helen to do. Her husband appeared to have forgotten the shameful fact of her adultery. He was treating her better than he had since the honeymoon. Bringing the painful memory back into his consciousness would probably rock the boat quite violently.

Content with things as they were, Helen avoided the question all Thursday night. She fretted over it all day Friday, finally deciding to mention it to Danny very casually while they watched TV that night. Her courage failed her. At breakfast on Saturday the invitation still remained unknown to Danny. It could wait no longer; the party was that night.

Helen drank her coffee and fidgeted until Danny's cup was less than half full. Not wanting to see Danny's face when she told him of the invitation, Helen took both cups over to the percolator. With her back to him, she fought to keep her voice nonchalant and told him they were invited to a party at the

Porters'. The instant and angry no that she expected never sounded.

In fact, there was an awkward pause of several seconds before Danny replied. When he did, it was to inquire if the party was to be another foursome or if others would also be present.

Four couples in all would be there, Helen told him, her hand trembling as she poured their cups full of coffee. No, she said in answer to his next question, she had nothing else planned. She was halfway back to the table when he gaily remarked that it sounded like a great idea and told her to accept. Helen had damn near dropped both cups of coffee right there on the floor.

Freshly showered and shaved, his hair combed and ready to get dressed, Danny came naked out of the bathroom. Helen was sitting on the side of the bed, her dress hiked up and one bare foot perched on the edge of the mattress. Four toenails boasted a still-wet coat of sexy pink polish. She dipped the small brush back into the bottle to carry polish to the nail of her big toe.

Danny went over and took the brush from her fingers. "Let me finish that for you," he offered, kneeling and beginning to paint on the polish before she could object.

His fingers teased ticklingly at the sloping

arch of her instep. "Don't, Danny, don't," she laughed. "Let me do it. You're going to mess it up."

Grinning up at her, he took a firmer hold of her foot and said, "I'll do it right, honey."

And he did. Nimbly he applied a pink coating to her toenail, biting his tongue in concentration all the while he guided the tiny brush. When the nail was covered, he backed away and turned her foot to admire his handiwork. "Good job, huh?"

After examining the results critically, she smiled back at him. "Yes, Rembrandt. It's a good job. Now give me the brush and get dressed while I do my other foot."

"I'll do it for you," he said seriously, putting her foot on the floor and raising the other. He placed the sole of her foot on his bare thigh and reached out to get more polish on the brush.

"But why? You've never offered to do my nails before."

"I dunno... just felt like it tonight."

"But I feel so silly with you kneeling there and painting my toenails. Don't you?"

"No. I don't see anything wrong with it," he returned, finishing the nail of her little toe and dipping back into the bottle for a new supply of polish. "Oh, I don't mean that anything is wrong with it. In fact, I kind of like it," Helen replied.

A nervous little smile played at Danny's mouth. "Make you feel good?"

"Yeah, as a matter of fact it does. Makes me feel rich... served. Be careful now. Don't smear it."

"Yes, ma'am."

The apprehension Helen had felt vanished. She felt in a teasing, playful mood. It was nice! She lay back luxuriously on the bed and sighed. "Tell you what, boy. Do a good job on my little piggies and I'll let you take over the job permanently."

She lay still, smiling contentedly as her husband painted the rest of her toenails. He took the bottle from her hand and capped it. Though her eyes were closed, she knew by the sound when Danny put the bottle on the nightstand. She thought it rather strange when he picked up her foot.

Then she felt his lips – on the sole of her foot! It was a long kiss, full of emotion! His lips were hot, passionate!

"Danny? Honey! What are you doing?"

He had a sheepish look on his face when Helen sat up, which only puzzled her all the more.

"There," he said, putting her foot down onto the floor. "All done."

He kept kneeling there, holding her foot and looking up at her questioning face. It embarrassed her. "You'd better get dressed," she admonished.

"Yeah. Guess so," he mumbled, reluctantly letting go of her foot.

He stood quickly and turned away from her to go over and get his shorts from the dresser. But he hadn't turned quickly enough to hide from Helen the cause of his sudden movement. Danny had a hard-on – painting her toenails had turned him on!

* * *

Neither Helen nor Danny were prepared for the sight which greeted them as the Porters' front door swung open. A lovely mulatto woman flashed them a warm smile. The fact that a Negress opened the door for them was in itself not unusual. Many of the more affluent citizens of Montgomery had maids. But this girl was obviously not a domestic servant. Girls as pretty as she could find far better jobs than the demeaning and small-paying position of maid. Besides, the Porters had no maid.

And this girl, even if they had hired a part-time maid just for the party, could not possibly be hired help. She was out of uniform – damn far out of uniform! The honey-brown face broke into an even wider smile at the Nielsens' mixed reactions. Both their mouths dropped open as they fought a losing battle and let their gazes fall to take in the exotic costume the Negress wore.

She was completely nude down to her small waist. Magnificent breasts stared back at them boldly, then seemed to mock the shocked expressions on their faces as the girl tried in vain to stifle a chuckle and could not keep the feminine globes from jiggling. A flowered sarong was draped about her full, womanly hips, with one side higher than the other. The slope of the garment's top cut just below a delicately indented belly-button. Her mirth caused the dark navel to jerk slightly back and forth. It seemed to be winking at them.

Sarong doesn't adequately describe the girl's flimsy covering. Mini-sarong would give a better picture. Its bottom hem came down almost halfway to her knees but an inverted V was cut in the front, its point stopping just barely below her pussy. Below the scanty costume two shapely, tan legs tapered to the floor and turned into dainty, bare feet with bright red toenails.

"You must be the Nielsens," the girl finally managed to say. "Come in, please. Maria's busy and asked me to get the door in her place."

"We were invited to a party here tonight," Helen mumbled, as she and Danny moved around the scantily-clad girl and into the foyer.

"You're at the right house," the girl assured them. She closed the door and snapped the lock. "I'm Ellie," she said, moving toward them gracefully.

Somewhat awkwardly, Danny introduced Helen and himself. He offered his hand and smiled, then appeared suddenly nervous when Ellie moved against him and kissed him instead of taking his hand.

"You're cute, Danny," she said as she stepped back. "Cute Southern white men have always been my greatest weakness."

Danny's collar got awfully tight as he glanced over at Helen. Her scowl bore into him, making him shift uneasily and clear his throat.

"Oh, don't misunderstand me, honey," Ellie said as she moved to Helen and kissed her, too. "It's the way they talk. I could listen to that drawl for days on end."

"Are you a party guest?" Helen asked. She felt like adding "or one of the hired help" after the way Danny responded to the dark girl. But she did not.

Helen bit her tongue. She hadn't told Danny about dancing with the handsome Negro. Lucky she hadn't let the catty remark slip out. From the semi-sweet tone of Ellie's answer she felt sure that she knew about it, and would probably be quite glad to let

Danny in on the secret. Helen forced a convincing smile. "I'm happy to know you, Ellie." Ellie kissed her again, this time letting her breasts brush intimately against Helen's. "You are a doll. Just as pretty as Maria said you were, and just as sweet. Come on," she said, taking both Danny and Helen by the hand, "let's join the party."

"It's down in the orgy r... in the rumpus room," she quickly corrected herself. "Watch your step, now," she advised, leading the way down the basement stairs.

"Maybe we ought to get ourselves home," Helen whispered.

"Why?"

"Did you hear what she almost said?"

"Probably just a joke. You know how people are."

Helen stopped in front of Danny on the stairs. "I don't know about that," she whispered, turning her head back toward him. "I've had a funny feeling about this party all along."

"Fer crissakes, Helen! Don't be such a silly little girl all your life!"

Danny's snorted response infuriated Helen. She shook his hand off her arm and clacked on down the stairs, not bothering to wait for him.

"Something wrong, baby?" Ellie stood waiting at the bottom of the stairs, smiling as she watched Helen's hips undulate toward her.

"No. Of course not," Helen said, coming up beside the dark, half-naked girl. "Let's go to the party."

Ellie led them across a bare concrete floor and opened a door in a panelled wall. Blinking at the dim, eerie, green lighting, Helen went through the door without bothering to check that Danny was following. She stopped inside the door, letting her eyes adapt to the dimness. The door closed behind her. The sound of the lock turning sent a stab of fear into her heart.

The whole thing looked and sounded so weird! The soft music was like nothing she'd ever heard before. Not music, not really. It was more like jungle drums beating in the distance, with hauntingly sensual little bursts of melodies from a flute breaking in now and then. It was a nice effect, though. She closed her eyes and swayed to the beat.

A woman moaned softly, then murmured so low that her words couldn't be made out. Helen opened her eyes and looked about the room. There was Buck, dancing with a white woman she had never seen before. Buck was wearing the same kind of little sarong that Ellie had on, and the girl nestled in his muscled arms wore a harem outfit. Maria stood behind the bar making drinks. Helen could only see the top of her outfit, a leather bra! The man helping her with the drinks was the other half of the harem girl. He looked as regal as a sultan, turban and all. And there, coming toward her, was Rod! His outfit was the weirdest of all – skintight black leather pants and a tapered leather shirt to match!

The woman sighed, then harshly sucked in her breath. It was part of the music! A man grunted. Old-fashioned bedsprings began to creak in time to the music. The beat speeded up, and the sighs and grunts and the creaking bedsprings grew more rapid. It was maddening!

Then Rod was standing in front of her, smiling as he took her into his arms and kissed her full on the lips. His tongue teased between her lips, darting back and forth in time to the frenzied sounds of the exotic music. The raspy bedsprings, the drums, the man grunting and the woman moaning orgasmically, the feel of leather under her clutching hands, Rod's tongue entering her mouth and darting about, his hands cupping her buttocks... too much! Too much!

The sound of male and female in the final throes of heated lovemaking bombarded Helen's ears. It caught her up and carried her along. She closed her eyes and clung weakly to Rod, returning his soul kiss and moaning with the girl on the record. She stood there trembling against him as the record ended.

Then he pulled away and held her out at arms length, smiling with satisfaction. "Welcome to the party, baby. How about a drink?"

Danny! Oh no! Not again! But she needn't have worried. Her husband was not behind her when she turned around. He was over near the bar, with Ellie. He had already shed his coat. They were sitting on a couch, looking into each other's eyes as Ellie removed his necktie.

"I think I need one... badly," she said.

"The fun is just beginning," Rod said laughingly, then took her hand and led her toward the bar.

"Glad you could make it, baby," Maria told her, coming out from behind the bar and kissing her on the mouth. "Here, they're all alike. Have one," she said, and pressed a cold glass into Helen's hand.

Nodding thanks, Helen sipped it gratefully. It was a margarita, the same as she'd had at the base on Monday. It was so cool and soothing that she turned it up and drank half of it down before she lowered the glass again. She looked down to see what else Maria had on. A leather miniskirt! And lace-up leather boots that came over the calves. The spike heels of the boots must be at least four inches, she decided. Maria unnerved her tonight. It wasn't only the outfit she wore. Something about her personality was different too – manlike, dominant. Helen got the same uneasy feeling she had when Maria had talked about all the power that Rod controlled when he flew the big bomber.

Maria grinned as she noticed Helen eyeing her leather garb. "Do you like it?"

"Well... it's a little far out for me. But it doesn't look bad on you. I don't know... leather."

"I love the feel of it on my bare skin," Maria admitted. "I don't have anything underneath... see?" She flipped up the tight leather skirt and held it.

"Maria!"

"What's the matter, baby? Cunt scare you?"

Amazed at herself, Helen stared down at Maria's crotch and let her take her hand and put it on her pubic mound. The crisp hair sent an electric-like shock through her body. Helen gasped and jerked her hand away. "Maria! For heaven's sake!"

"Sorry, baby. I didn't mean to shock you, but it won't bite, you know." Maria smiled and put her skirt down. "Come on. Let me introduce you around."

The sultan was named Harold. He was very polite. Almost shy. They shook hands and mumbled the proper amenities. Then Maria took her over to where Buck and the harem girl were still dancing.

Buck smiled intimately at her and squeezed her hand. "Save me a dance," he said.

The harem girl was in fact Harold's wife. Her name was Bess. A nod and a "glad to know you" was all Helen got from her. Bess had a yearning look in her eye. "Where's Sam?" she asked Maria.

"Don't worry, honey. You'll get Sam," Maria promised.

"But where is he? I haven't seen him around," Bess whined.

"When the time is right!" Maria snapped. "Now shut up about it. Rod will go for Sam when I'm good and ready, and not before. Now don't bug me about it any more!"

"Sure, Maria, sure," Bess hastened to agree, her face mirroring fear as she shrank away. She went to the bar for a drink.

"Who's Sam?" Helen wanted to know.

Buck laughed. "You'll see. Maria likes to spring Sam as a surprise guest. He really livens up a dying party, doesn't he, Lash?"

Maria's eyes twinkled. "Bess goes for that type of entertainment. She's the one that livens it up more than Sam."

Sam? Lash? What type of entertainment? What was going on? Helen had to ask. "What kind of party is this, Maria?"

"All for fun, baby. All for fun."

"You could have at least told me it was

going to be a costume party. Everyone's in costume except Danny and me."

"I don't think your husband's noticed that yet, Helen," Buck commented as he glanced across the room.

Sure enough, Danny hadn't noticed. Helen followed Buck's approving stare and saw Danny and Ellie still sitting on the couch. They were embracing passionately, their open mouths glued together and their hands eagerly fondling genitals that were exposed for all to see. Her cheeks flushing with embarrassment, Helen jerked her head back around.

"Helen's noticed, though," Maria said. "She should have a costume. Don't you think she'd feel more at home if she had an appropriate costume for the party, Buck?"

"Of course she would, Maria. Why don't you loan her your red outfit?"

"Oh no, Buck. Those leather riding britches would look tacky on Helen. She's much too feminine for that kind of get-up."

"No," Helen protested weakly. "I don't really need a costume."

A male voice came from behind her. "Only way to feel at home is to have a costume that fits the mood."

Helen swung around to see Rod leering at her. "All right. Let me run home and see... I think I have one packed away." She had no intention of coming back, at least not tonight. Once out of the door the party would be over, as far as she was concerned. She was beginning to realise what the so-called party would turn into, and she wanted no part of it.

Rod shook his head. "Huh-uh. Too late."

Panic welled up and made it hard for Helen to breathe. She looked to Buck, searching for an ally. But he only shrugged his broad shoulders and grinned. She wheeled around to face Maria. "What does he mean, Maria? How can it be too late when I only live right across the street?"

"This is a special kind of party, little one. Once all the guests have arrived, no one leaves until the rest are ready to break it up."

"Then... you're not going to let me go? Do you think you can keep me here against my will? No! I won't have it! I'm not going to stay for your party. I'm walking out. Danny can do whatever he pleases, but I'm saying good night!"

With that, Helen whirled and ran over to the door. Frantically she searched it for a knob. There was none on the inside, only a place for a key, and the door swung into the room. The key. It was the only way to get out of the room. Ellie had it. Anyway, she was the one who let them in and locked the door. She hurried over to the sofa.

Danny didn't see her approach. He was bent over sucking on one of Ellie's brown tits. Her legs were spread apart, and Danny had two fingers working energetically in and out of her slippery, dark cunt. How could he? How could he fall in so quickly and eagerly with this type of people?

But Danny was not at the moment her main concern. The key. That's what she wanted, in order to escape this insane party. Helen bent over Ellie and called her name.

Brown eyelids came open lazily, revealing glassy and widely dilated brown eyes. Ellie focused with difficulty, smiling when she recognised Helen. She licked her lips. "Come on in, baby. The water's fine and I've got enough lovin' for you too. Kiss me," she sultrily invited, pursing her lips and closing her eyes again.

"The key!" Helen demanded. "Give me the key!"

"You wanna leave?" Ellie sounded as if she were astounded and burst into a fit of laughter. Danny raised his head and frowned, then went back to sucking the pouting nipple as if he hadn't even seen her.

"What the hell's so funny about that?"

"Relax, baby, relax. Let your hair down and enjoy it. He is," Ellie said, nodding to Danny's nuzzling head. "Force yourself if you have to at first. You'll come to like it. I did. Might as well. Maria hides the one key. My first party I looked for it for over an hour. Didn't find it. You won't either. Join in!"

Chapter 5

Stamping angrily over to the bar, Helen picked up another drink. She sipped gingerly at it, her eyes all the while searching for a possible hiding place for the key. It was no use. The key could be anywhere. There were thousands of places about the room where such a small article could be hidden. The anger within her rushed out suddenly, a sense of helplessness replacing it. How could Danny do this to her? She felt like crying.

But no. No, by God! She'd show Danny. Two could play at that game. She'd pretend to go along with the mood of the party. Maybe if she made a spectacle of herself he would come to his senses and do something to get them both out of there before it turned into an all-out orgy.

How to do it? It had to be something that Danny wouldn't like her to do, something really far out that would shame him. He hadn't liked the nude swimming, not at all. That was it! She'd put on a show – a strip tease. Danny wouldn't like her doing that in front of the other men, he especially wouldn't want her taking off her clothes in front of Buck. Yes. She'd play up to the Negro. Danny certainly wouldn't be able to sit there calmly and watch her run her white hands all over that brown skin. That would bring him to his senses in a hurry!

"Hey!" she yelled. "Everybody look this way. Look at me!" She watched the seven faces turn one by one toward her. She shivered. All those eyes! Danny looked puzzled. The other six merely smiled, waiting amusedly to see what was coming.

"This party's gettin' boring," she announced, looking directly at Maria. "You're the hostess. Can't you liven it up so we can all have a good time?"

Maria and Rod glanced at each other. Both shrugged. "What'd you have in mind, baby?" asked Maria.

"Entertainment."

Maria laughed. "You'll get all the 'entertainment' you want before it's over."

"I feel like doing a little entertaining myself," Helen replied, putting down her drink and going over to where Maria, Rod and Buck still stood. She stopped in front of them and put her hands on her hips, standing with her feet apart.

"What'd you have in mind, eager beaver?" Rod asked with a grin.

"Him," she shot back, stepping up to Buck. She undid the catch of his sarong and whisked it off, pitching it away and leaving him stark naked. Looking up into his eyes, Helen put her hands on his chest and began stroking down his body in a circular motion. As she went lower, her eyes followed the movement of her hands. When she got to his hips and lower abdomen, she stopped short. The size of his organ, which was slowly rearing up its purplish-brown, circumcised head, made her gasp aloud .It was the third dick she had ever seen, and by far the biggest! Buck was as much bigger than Rod as Rod was bigger than Danny! The rising column of black penis sent a shiver shooting through Helen. The thought of even trying to accommodate such a monster struck fear in her.

No. She mustn't show it. Act calm. That was the thing to do. It couldn't possibly go that far. Danny wouldn't let it. He would never stand for a black guy doing it to her – never! But she had to tease Danny and make him think she might like it to happen. Then he'd make Maria and Rod come up with the key and they'd go home.

She put her palms on Buck's chest and pushed him back a step. Grinning up at his face, she said, "Later for you, daddy. Right now I want to dance, and get out of these street clothes at the same time. Maria, you got a record to strip by?"

Maria had a puzzled frown on her face. She made fists and put them on her hips. "Well, I'll be damned!"

"Be anything you want," Helen retorted.

"Innocent little Helen wants to strip for us. I just don't believe it," Maria remarked.

"If you've got a suitable record, put it on. Then you'll damn well believe it," Helen came back quickly. She tried to sound flippant, hoping that Danny would get the idea she really meant to take off all her clothes in front of these people. She didn't want to. She didn't think she'd have to, as Danny would surely stop her before she was completely naked.

Danny sat beside a grinning Ellie, his scowl warning Helen not to do it. She smiled and winked at her husband, then put her hands behind her head and hunched her pelvis his way. It almost worked. Danny started to say something to her. But he failed to follow through. Instead, he dropped his gaze from her face, embarrassed by the laughter which Helen's little hunch evoked from the others.

Maria's voice ordered rather than requested. "Bess. Put an appropriate record on for our would-be stripper. You know the one," Maria added, sure that Bess recalled her first party, the one at which she'd forced the young woman to strip against her will.

Danny sat stunned, watching as Bess broke into a little giggle and hurried over to the record player. What had come over Helen to make her act this way? For that matter, what had come over him, he wondered. True, he had been secretly hoping that Rod would somehow manage to screw Helen again. But this party! It was going to turn into an all-out orgy for sure! He hadn't expected this, not with strangers. With only Rod and Maria was he willing to let things take their course, not with these other people. And that big black guy. Why, Helen was teasing him! Leading him on!

There she stood now, letting Buck hug her from the back and cup her tits. Why, she was smiling right at him, her own husband, and rotating her butt against that big, black cock! It was more than Danny could endure. "Helen! Stop it!"

She only smiled the more. "Why, darling? We came to a party. Aren't you supposed to have fun at a party?" She stepped to the side, her eyes leading Danny's to the massive black organ boldly standing out from Buck's groin. Her fingers trembling slightly, Helen reached out and took it in her hand. It was thick and hot to her touch! So sturdy was Buck's rod that she discovered to her horror the impossibility of encircling it completely with her grasping fingers. "You found your fun, Danny. Now look at what's going to give me mine," she said, her voice quavering with a mixture of fear and the beginnings of desire.

"I'll be damned if it is!" Danny shouted, jumping threateningly to his feet. He looked so silly, thought Helen. There he is, as mad as hell at the idea of me with Buck, and his stupid dick is hard and poking out of his open fly. It was what she had wanted, yet somehow it seemed so ridiculous. He just stood there, glowering at her with his thing pointed her way. She laughed. She couldn't help it.

"We're going home," Danny growled, stamping across the room toward her. "Right now!"

But Maria hurried out to meet him in the centre of the room. "Cool it, Danny. Be a good boy and go sit back down with Ellie."

"Piss on you," Danny snapped, reaching out his arm to sweep Maria out of his way.

It all happened so fast. Maria's hands shot up and grabbed his arm. With lightning speed she moved and drew him with her. Her foot came between his legs. A split second later a sharp pain numbed his arm. He was falling suddenly. The next thing he knew he was on the floor. A pain in his neck was added to the one in his tautly bent-back arm.

Pussy greeted his eyes as he looked up. Maria was standing over him, one foot on the floor and the other pressing into his throat. Those heels! God, how that spike heel dug into his soft flesh! With his free hand Danny clutched at the lace-up boot. He grasped her ankle and tried to push the painful foot away. It was no use. The boot only bit into his throat more painfully than before. Groaning aloud, he looked up to plead for mercy. Maria's expression filled him with sudden terror. She was demented, her face a mask of sadistic evil!

"That's it, baby! Fight me! Fight me!"

"Aargh! Uung!" The pain was unbearable. Danny released her ankle and opened his mouth to speak, to beg her to quit hurting him so. Only a gurgle came from his mouth. Her foot prevented the formation of words.

"You're helpless, Danny. Do you hear me? Helpless!"

Danny tried to speak. He could not. He closed his eyes and moaned. Her face! It was so evil, so distorted! He couldn't stand to look at it.

"Slap the floor once if you understand me, Danny." She waited until he weakly hit the floor one time with his free hand. "Good. Now hear me well. I'm taking you over. You're nothing but a puny runt. All you're fit to be is a slave. I'm making you my slave. Do you understand?"

Again Danny forced himself to open his eyes. He gawked up incredulously at Maria's face. She had to be kidding. This couldn't be for real. "Noo-oo," he said, struggling against the pressure of her foot to get the simple syllable out. Then he winced in agony, croaking pitifully as she bore down brutally on his throat.

Helen ran toward them, screaming, "Maria! For God's sake, stop it! You're hurting him! Stop it, Maria! Stop it!"

But she got nowhere. Rod grabbed her from behind and dragged her back before she took three steps. He twisted one arm up behind her back till she was whimpering in pain.

"Helen? Listen to me, sweetie. I don't want to have to hurt you," he said, trying to calm her.

"Turn me loose," Helen whimpered. "Get Maria off Danny. She's killing him! Killing him..."

"No, Helen, she's not killing him," Rod assured. "Hurting him, yes, but not permanently."

"Make her stop, Rod... make her stop. Please!"

"No. She needs this. I won't make her stop."

"I don't know what you're talking about. Maybe Maria needs it, but what about Danny? He's in agony! Who needs that?"

"Shut up, Helen," hissed Maria. "Just shut up... or you'll get some of the same!"

"No! Turn me loose!" Helen yelled, trying to wrench free of Rod's hold.

"Okay, baby, if you won't listen to reason," Rod grunted, managing to restrain the struggling Helen.

One leather-covered arm came about Helen's waist and locked vice-like, squeezing the breath out of her. Fingers clutched at the bodice of her dress and ripped off the buttons. Then Rod's hand was on her bare skin, his fingers tearing away her bra. A breast was cupped, examined by groping fingertips. The fingertips found their mark, the tender brown areola and the prominent nipple at its end.

Knowing what was coming, Helen gritted her teeth. The fingers moved to better advantage, rolling and pulling her nipple out in order to get a firmer hold. Then it began, slowly at first. Little by little Rod's fingertips, clamped down on her sensitive sex flesh. It was almost pleasant at the start, like a light caress that grew steadily heavier and heavier. Then, when the pressure increased to a certain point, the caress turned into a minor source of irritation. From that it grew into a faint pain, felt as pain but not really anything to become alarmed over.

Helen had almost decided that Rod was

merely using the threat of ill treatment to keep her from trying to rescue Danny, when he whispered in her ear, "Brace yourself, sweetie. It may get a little rough from here on. If you feel like screaming, let it out. No one but us revellers will hear you, though, and it only incites us on to bigger and better things. Anyway, the room is soundproofed. So suit yourself."

Then it began. The pain increased just as slowly as it had up to that point. But with one difference – it had now passed the threshold of tolerability. It could no longer be ignored. Some acknowledgement of its presence had to be made. Helen's upper lip began to tremble. She sucked in her breath and tried to wriggle loose. But Rod was too strong, and he had her arms pinned to her sides so that she couldn't use her hands to try and pull his pinching fingers from her breast.

Maria had stopped her mistreatment of Danny and was looking on with interest, her foot still holding him to the floor helplessly as Rod worked on Helen. The sight caused her nostrils to flare as she excitedly licked at her parted lips. "God, baby," she said to Rod. "The way you bring it on so slowly is pure torture for me. You know that, don't you, you lovely bastard?"

"You're always so eager, Maria, my pet. It's

downright crude the way you hurt your sex objects so quickly. You're the worst kind of sadist, my sweet. You give your victims no chance to respond, no time to come to enjoy the pain you inflict upon them."

"I'll improve, Rod. I promise. Danny gave me no choice. I had to take him out of action."

"All right, sweetheart. I agree to that. Forget it now, and watch closely. Look at Helen's face. See how she's licking her lips and squinting her eyes? She doesn't want to let on that I'm hurting her. And I'm not, not really. It started as a lover's tender caress, an enjoyable thing to all. Pleasure. That was the first thing she felt. That's an important conditioning factor, Maria.

"If you want a willing subject, you simply have to give them pleasure at the very first. Then increase the pleasure bit by bit. Look at her now. See how her mouth hangs open? Hear the urgency of her laboured breathing? I'm pinching her tit quite harshly now but she still perceives it as pleasure. Had I started at this level of intensity she would've immediately experienced sharp pain. It would have been unbearable. Probably she would have screamed in protest."

Strange, thought Helen, how Rod's voice seemed to come from a distance. He hadn't moved. He was still behind her, still holding her to him. His voice was soft in her ear, talking only to her now, "Helen? Close your eyes, Helen."

She felt so helpless, so small and weak. Already she had ceased to struggle, had accepted the fact that Rod would do with her as he pleased. "Yes," she whispered, nodding agreement as her eyelids came down slowly and shut out the pitiful sight of her husband lying beneath Maria's boot. Struggling hadn't helped Danny. Maria, a woman only little larger than herself, had reduced him to a state of degradation. How could she hope to prevent Rod from having his way? Did she even want to stop him, she wondered dimly. This thing he was doing to her. It hurt... yet it didn't hurt. There was more pleasure than pain in it.

Rod began talking to her now, very softly, very comfortingly. He was careful not to increase the pressure on her nipple, and merely kept it constant. The monotone of his voice helped her to relax as the nerves in her sensitive brown nipple adapted. Bit by bit the pain ebbed until Helen hazily wondered if his fingers still held her nipple captive. She moved her chest a fraction of an inch to the left in order to determine for sure if her nipple was still being pinched. It was. The tiny spear of pain told her beyond a doubt. She sighed.

"Helen?"

It was Rod's voice. "Yes?"

"How do you feel, baby?"

"So strange," she murmured. "So calm... so contented... so accepting."

"Am I hurting you?"

"No... not now."

"I'm going to hurt you some more. You know that, don't you?"

"Yes, I know. I want you to. If you'll do it slowly like you have till now, I won't resist you."

"Do you like what I've done to you so far?"

"Oh yesss... I do!"

"Good. I thought you would. There's one thing we have to settle before we go on, though."

"What is it, darling?

"About your husband. He belongs to Maria just as you now belong to me. You will both enjoy the party much more if you accept that fact. Will you put yourself completely in my hands, Helen?"

"Yes. I put myself completely in your hands. I will do as you wish," Helen whispered. She had no choice and knew it. But she did not want to resist, not now. Her intuition told her that anything Rod did to her would somehow turn into pleasure for both of them. "I belong to you... Danny belongs to Maria. But..."

"She will not cause him any permanent

physical damage. Is that what you're worried about?"

"Yes. I couldn't stand for that to happen. I love him."

"Then relax. Maria knows intuitively about men. She assures me that Danny will soon voluntarily submit himself to her will, just as you have submitted to me. Can we continue now?"

"Please," Helen said, then gasped out loud as he suddenly released the pressure on her nipple. A million tiny, tingling arrows shot into her breast. It was the reverse of pain, the return to a normal state. I don't like that," she moaned.

"Open your eyes, Helen. I want you to take off all your clothes," Rod said, removing his arms from around her body and stepping away.

Reluctantly she opened her eyes and began undoing the remaining buttons down the front of her dress. She saw Danny, still lying on the floor. Ellie and Bess were removing his clothes as Maria stood over all three of them with a whip held threateningly in her hand. Evidently Danny had accepted his fate, for he made no effort to prevent what was going on.

"Maria was right about your husband, wasn't she?" asked Rod as he came up beside Helen.

"He has a hard-on. She must have been

right," Helen agreed, stepping out of her dress and draping it across Rod's proffered arm.

Chapter 6

She stood with her legs apart, one hand made into a fist and resting on her hip, the other rocking a coiled whip back and forth through the air. The hard sole and spike heel of her boot had left a steady pain in Danny's throat. Every beat of his heart seemed to throb there, reminding him that she would stop at nothing to master him. It was utterly humiliating to lie at her feet and allow the two women to strip off his clothes as Maria had ordered them to do. Yet he dared not protest.

Fear of what might come flooded his mind. Common sense told him that Maria was demented, that she meant him no good. He wanted out of this place and away from her. But how? How? Did he dare try to get to his feet again?

No. Once was enough! He'd already attempted to get up, when Maria had taken her foot from his throat. What a mistake that had been! His scalp still ached from the vicious way she'd grabbed a handful of hair and jerked him roughly onto his back again. Then the boot... right back onto his gasping throat! Maria had threatened to kill him then, had squatted down close and hissed it into his face. Slave, she'd called him, slave! Then she'd spat in his face and dared him to try and get up again before she told him it was permissible to do so.

Something inside Danny had wilted when Maria's sputum hit and spattered over his face. All hope of complete escape died at that very moment. Maria had watched his expression change, grinning satanically above him and laughing deep within her throat. She'd known then. They both had. She was Mistress, he slave. He was going to do as she ordered, one way or another. She was the stronger willed, the dominant one, the Supreme Female. His prick growing hard at the thought, he wondered if Maria might let him lick her boots. He'd opened his mouth to ask and got a slap across the face before the first word formed.

One shoe came off as Bess pulled, then the other. His socks followed. Her eager hands gripped the cuffs of his trousers and tugged them down, dragging his shorts half off before the pants slid on down his legs and over his feet. Straddle-legged, Bess walked on her knees back up to his midsection. Her fingernails dug sharply into his skin as she hooked trembling fingers over the waistband of his shorts. She jerked at first one side and then the other, working them down over his hips and buttocks.

His stiff dick flipped free and slapped against his lower abdomen. Oh God! If only Helen weren't here! She shouldn't see this, he thought. What would she think of him? How could he face her after this?

Raising only his head, he saw her across the room and gasped. She was taking her own clothes off. From the looks of it, she was not being forced to, but stripping of her own free will! Her dress was already off. Rod had it draped over his arm. He was smiling at her as she worked her slip up over her hips and breasts. It went over her head, leaving her in only a tattered bra, panties, hose and high-heeled shoes. She hung the slip over Rod's arm with the dress, then turned for him to unsnap her bra.

Gone now were his shorts. Ellie was sitting on his thighs, pulling his arms and urging him to sit up. He looked up at Maria, his eyes silently asking if he should. Maria nodded. He let Ellie pull him into a sitting position and push his shirt back and down his arms. Her deft fingers found the bottom of his T-shirt and slipped it over his head as he raised his arms to help.

There he sat, naked, watching his wife

wiggle out of her panties with Rod waiting to take them from her. Even under these circumstances Helen looked like an angel. The hair at the edge of her pussy looked damp. Danny knew his wife was aroused. It excited him to see that she was. He felt an urge to go over to her, to kneel between her legs and lick her cunt.

A hiss sounded behind him, a crack. Leather thongs bit into his bare back. Yelping at the unexpected blow, Danny winced in pain and jumped up. He got as far as his knees when the whip cut into his flesh the second time. The blow was harder than the first, sending him off to the side and falling back to the floor. He rolled onto his back, staring up as Maria loomed above him with the whip poised once more. With an insane look on her face, she brought it down expertly across his stomach. He screamed in agony, writhing as Maria drew the snake-like leather rope slowly across his skin.

She teased him with it now, stroking the flexible whip back and forth across his stomach. Danny glanced down and saw the red welt her blow had caused. His hand caught at the torture instrument in an effort to wrest it from her. Both his hands claimed it, pulling it from her as she struggled to hang on.

He seemed to be winning. Maria was

weaker than he was, after all. Using all his strength, Danny pulled the whip hand over hand, dragging a furious Maria ever closer to him. He had all the flexible part of the whip now in his possession. The stiff handle was only about eighteen inches long. Maria clung tenaciously to her end, digging the spike heels of her boots into the carpeted floor and throwing the muscles of her legs into the struggle.

"Stop it, Danny! You'd better quit fighting me if you know what's good for you!" Maria barked.

Her hands were sliding up the shaft inch by inch. Finally Danny had it all but the small portion her hands covered. The very end of the whip handle was made in the shape of a phallus. To that Maria clung, the bulbous leather glans alone showing on her side of her hands.

A gleam coming to her eyes, Maria braced herself as if she intended to exert all her power in one final effort to reclaim the whip from Danny. Using leg, back and arm muscles, she wiped the smile from Danny's face by gaining back several inches of the handle. When he countered with all his might, Maria merely let go of the handle and laughed out loud as Danny hit himself in the mouth with the cock head.

While he was still seeing stars, she acted.

The toe of her boot caught him directly in the butt. He wailed out and rolled onto his back. That's what she had been waiting for. Maria let out a squeal of joy as she jumped in the air and landed with both feet planted firmly on Danny's chest.

"No, Maria... noo," Danny pleaded.

But it did him no good. Her face glowing evilly, Maria jumped up and down on Danny's body. Her spike heels dug into his flesh brutally, leaving red splotches to mark where she'd walked upon him in utter domination. "Slave! Slave! Slave!" she chanted.

"Yes... yes, you win, Maria. Aargh! Stop... please stop!"

Coming to a stop at the top of his chest, Maria spat down into Danny's face. "Pig! When you wish to address me, you'll call me Mistress!"

"Yes, Maria... I mean, Mistress Maria."

"That's better, dog. Now... what are you whining about?"

"I can't take it any more... Mistress. Please stop, please."

"Is the filthy swine begging for mercy? Well, are you?"

"Yes, Mistress... mercy. Dear God, have mercy!"

Quickly she squatted and slapped his face several times. "I am your God! If there is any mercy, I alone will give it. Do not call any name other than mine... understand?"

"Yes, Mistress Maria... Yes."

"Lie still now. I have decided to favour you," Maria said to Danny, then turned and called for a washcloth.

In the back of the room was a partitioned cubicle enclosing a shower stall, a commode, and a wash basin. Bess, herself excited over the way Maria had mastered Danny so quickly, hurried into the bathroom and dampened a washcloth. She half-ran across the room in her eagerness to please Maria. "Here, Mistress. Here is the cloth," she breathed.

Smiling sweetly at Bess, Maria said, "Well? Don't just stand there, you stupid little bitch! Wash his face!"

Licking her lips, Bess dropped to her knees and began rubbing the wet cloth over Danny's face. "Are you going to do him the highest honour, Mistress? May I get my face up close and see it if you do?" she asked nervously.

Maria reached out and pinched harshly at Bess' cheek, wringing her flesh until Bess began to whimper. "How many times must I tell you, bitch? When I want any suggestions from you, I'll ask for them." Maria gave her cheek a final twist before she let go.

"I was just asking... that's all, Mistress," Bess whined.

"I haven't decided yet! If I do, then you can watch up close. Haven't you finished cleaning his face?"

"All done," Bess beamed, running the damp cloth up Danny's face as she scooted backward out of Maria's way. "Shall Ellie and I assist you?"

"Yes, and Harold, too. You all know what I expect of you."

Ellie and Bess each took one of Danny's arms and stretched it out to the side. Then they squatted with one foot on his wrists and one on the back of his palm-down hands. Harold waddled over and plopped his fat butt down on Danny's thighs. He sat just above the knees, one leg on either side of Danny's and facing up toward Maria's back.

"He's got a lovely peter," Harold exclaimed, leaning over till his face almost touched the head of Danny's semi-rigid organ.

"You can suck it if you want to, Harold," Maria told him matter-of-factly. "Just so you keep his legs pinned to the floor."

It was all the encouragement that plump Harold needed. He heaved a satisfied sigh and shifted himself to lower his mouth over Danny's cock. His cheeks hollowed. His eyes closed contentedly. With one hand on the floor beside Danny's left buttock and the other beside his right, Harold started doing four inch push-ups from his waist up, sucking and slurping as his head rose and fell.

Looking up in wide-eyed confusion, Danny moaned, "Make him quit... don't let him do that!"

"Pay it no heed, slave. I have a treat for you that will make you forget what Harold is doing," Maria said.

She stood up with her feet still on his chest, then stepped off with a foot on either side of his head. Hiking up her leather skirt, she squatted down again and brought her crotch hovering over his face. "Look at it," she ordered. "Look closely and study every inch. Are you looking?"

"I'm looking," Danny answered, his voice quavering a bit.

"Wash it," she ordered. "Use your tongue. Get it nice and clean from one end to the other. Lick gently. I don't want to feel your teeth at all. If I do, you may regret it. A tongue bath makes me purr like a kitten. But teeth... don't let me know you even have teeth or I'll piss right in your mouth. Got it?"

"Oh God," Danny moaned.

"There you go again," Maria snapped, reaching down and twisting his ears painfully. "I told you that I'm your God. Don't forget it again! Now... lick me," she hissed, and pulled his face against her crotch by the ears.

Coarse cunt hair mashed against Danny's

lips. He opened his mouth and probed out with his tongue. Maria tasted strong, unclean. She smelled of urine and sweat allowed to accumulate for several days. He gagged and drew his tongue back into his mouth.

"Lick! Lick, you bastard!"

He did. He was afraid not to. Maria had made her threats good as far as he had tested them. There was no doubt in his mind that she wouldn't hesitate to urinate over his face if he displeased her.

"That's it, Danny. That's a good slave. A little farther... put your tongue up my cunt a little farther... oohh... nice, nice. Wiggle it around now. That's it! Fine. More!"

The mouth on Danny's dick was beginning to feel good. Maria made so many demands on him, kept him so busy licking and tonguing her pussy that he almost forgot it was a man's mouth working at him. That tongue spinning around the crown of his dick! The suction – so harsh at times that cheeks pressed softly and hotly along his shaft! Smothering... Maria had her cunt over his nose now, as well as his mouth. Some of her juices got sucked up his nostrils as he tried desperately to breathe. Coughing and spluttering, Danny managed to turn his head enough to the side to catch a much needed breath.

"Did I feel teeth, slave? Did I?" Maria demanded angrily.

"No, Mistress... no, I'm being very careful so that you will not."

"Get back at it, then. Half your job is now finished. Well done so far, slave. Now, here is your reward!"

Wiggling forward, Maria brought her asshole to his mouth. Surely she doesn't expect that, thought Danny. She couldn't expect him to do that!

But she did, and said so in no uncertain terms. "Lick my ass, slave. Consider it your dessert. Gently now. The tip of your worthless tongue first. Do it well. I leave you to wonder what will happen if you don't."

"Do it anyway," Bess pleaded. "Right in his mouth... do it, do it now! Men are such shitty creatures anyhow. Make him eat a turd as it comes out of your asshole. I wanna see it..."

"Shut up, Bess! One more word out of you and I'll make you suck his ass!"

Bess turned as white as a sheet at even the thought of putting her mouth to a male's anus. Mouthing a hasty agreement, she shut her mouth and kept it closed, gladly.

"Now, Danny," Maria said. "Go at it nice and easy."

It wasn't nearly as repulsive as Danny had expected. The odour and strong taste of Maria's unwashed pussy had dulled his taste buds to the point that he barely distinguished the flavour of shit. He detected a heady muskiness, nothing more, and decided that Maria must have left only her cunt unwashed for his degradation. Slowly he licked back and forth at the crack of her ass, letting the tip of his tongue jab a little deeper up into her asshole each time he passed it. It seemed to please her immensely.

"That's it, baby," she murmured softly, "That's it. Good. Very good. More tongue. Give me a little more."

Suddenly he wanted to please her very much. It was important to him that she feel pleasure. Serving her seemed right and natural, a part of him that she had brought awake. Being extra careful not to let his teeth touch her flesh, Danny tightened his lips around her quivering anus. Alternately he sucked gently at the brown hole and jabbed in deep with his tongue. Her moans of pleasure spurred him on.

Doing her ass wasn't enough. She was Supreme, his Mistress. His cock threatened to explode inside Harold's suctioning mouth. Extending his tongue to full length, Danny began to rock his head wildly back and forth, licking her asshole up to her cunt, flicking her clitoris and then hurrying back to her anus.

"Oh, Danny!" Maria exclaimed breathlessly. "You're doing a wonderful job!

Keep it up... keep it up and I'll make you the favourite of all my slaves," she promised, stiffening above his head and shutting her eyes as orgasm drew near.

Soft, spit-slick female crotch began to quiver out of control as Danny went on licking furiously. Anything she wanted to do was now all right with Danny, anything at all. Nothing was too good for her or too vile and belittling for him. He began muttering incoherently as he licked and jabbed with his tongue, urging Maria to defile him, to piss on him, to expel a turd and mash it into his mouth, to come and press her fluttering cunt tightly over his face, to smother him as she climaxed.

Though his words were too jumbled to make out, Maria knew from past experience what he was trying to tell her. As the first waves of orgasm shot out through her sweaty loins, she ground her cunt cruelly down over his face and pinned his head to the floor. Then, quaking in every extremity of her body, she hunched her crotch up and down, rubbing it over his entire face.

Cunt covered his eyes, asshole claimed the tip of his nose. Back down. Cunt over his nose. Clitoris flipping from side to side over the bridge of his nose just below his eyes. Asshole at his mouth, demanding a worshipful tongue be inserted as far as possible. Hot, wet mouth on his cock. Maria wailed out above him, proclaiming her shuddering orgasm for all to see and hear. He couldn't breathe, was being smothered. His cock exploded and sent jet after jet of hot come spiralling into the sucking mouth. Grunting. Fighting for air. A long time. Then it was over and Maria was rolling off his face as the mouth left his cock.

Danny lay gasping desperately for breath, dimly aware that Maria was speaking to him. Finally he was able to make out her words. She wanted him to get up, to accompany her. Ellie and Bess helped him get weakly to his feet. Meekly he followed Maria to the back of the room, his knees threatening to buckle with each step he took. She opened a door for him. He went through it. It was a bathroom, and Maria was coming in with him. He turned to tell her that he needed no help, that he could manage for himself.

She paid him no heed. Taking his cock in her hand, she held it while he relieved himself into the commode. When he was finished, she led him by the cock into the shower stall. "I'm going to give you a nice warm shower," she murmured softly. "Sit down in the centre of the shower."

"Sit down?"

"Sit down," she urged, pressing his shoulders until he obeyed. "Now. Put your arms around your knees and hold them up to your chest."

It seemed a strange way to take a shower, but he did as she directed. What was she doing? One booted foot came on either side of his buttocks. Leather rustled softly. Her smooth thighs brushed at his shoulders, then pulled out to the sides.

"Look up, Danny," she coaxed.

He turned up his face obediently. Cunt met his gaze. She was standing over him, with her cunt just a scant few inches above his face. The lips of her lovely cunt relaxed and appeared to open slightly. Then it came bursting forth as Maria laughed insanely above him. Hot and yellow and smelly! Urine! Gushing in torrents from her pussy and hitting directly into his face. He moaned mournfully, then opened his mouth.

The warm, yellow stream dwindled to a trickle, then stopped entirely. Maria stepped from the shower. She was a blur, a ghostly outline. Danny's eyes burned something fierce. He sat there in a huddle, drenched and smelly, waiting for Maria to tell him he could get up. Water sounded in the sink, then stopped.

He could see better now, well enough to make out that she was washing the insides of her thighs and boots with a washcloth. Water sounded again before she rubbed the cloth back and forth over her crotch.

She came to the edge of the shower stall. The cloth hit him in the face and fell onto his knees.

"You're a sickening sight," she hissed. "Get up. Take a shower. When you're presentable again, come and find me. I've got more plans for you. Any objections, slave?"

"No, Mistress... none," he mumbled.

Her hand reached in and spun the cold water on to full force. It beat down on him, making him shiver and his teeth chatter as she jerked the shower curtain closed.

"Brush your teeth, too," she snapped. "There are extra brushes in the medicine cabinet."

Then her silhouette faded from the curtain. The spike heels of her boots sounded on the tiled floor. The door opened. It closed with a bang, leaving Danny alone and wondering if he were completely insane.

The thought still plagued him several minutes later. He stood at the bathroom door, showered, teeth brushed, dried and clean. Why was he going back out to Maria? Why was his heart beating faster as he wondered what she had in store for him next? It was unfathomable, yet so simple. She was his Mistress and he was her slave. She ordered, and he now willingly obeyed. Accepting it with a sigh, Danny opened the door and went in search of Maria, ready and eager to submit to whatever evil scheme lurked in the depths of her devilish mind.

All of them, his wife, Helen, included, were clustered around a table. Each sipped at a drink and smoked a cigarette. He wondered at that. Helen had never smoked a whole cigarette by herself. Occasionally she took his and indulged in a puff or two, that was all. But now she had one going all to herself. It was a bad habit. He didn't want his wife to take it up. He bit his tongue. Now was not the time to complain about it.

He saw that they'd saved a chair for him as he neared the table. A drink was also waiting, he noticed, and a cigarette. Maybe his ordeal was over. Perhaps it had been an initiation, or something like that.

"Have a chair, Danny," Rod said amiably.

Danny stopped behind the empty chair. Helen was sitting next to Rod, between him and the big black man. Her eyes looked different, funny. She smiled at him and half giggled. Danny mistakenly assumed she was laughing at what had happened to him. She had seen it, all of it except the part in the shower, and Maria had probably told them all about that. He couldn't meet her gaze. Mumbling a thank you to Rod, he lowered his eyes and took his seat.

Looking down at the table, he picked up his

drink and took a deep pull. The cigarette struck him as odd when he put down the drink beside it. It was handmade, rolled in brown paper.

"Smoke your cigarette, Danny," Maria said, her voice hostess-warm now. "It'll make the world look like a better place in a jiffy. I guarantee it."

He picked it up and held it between thumb and forefinger, examining it closely. He knew what it was now. Once or twice he'd seen cigarettes like this one when he was in the navy. "Pot?" he asked.

"The best you can get," Buck said, grinning and slurring his words slightly. "A civilian friend of mine gets it for me when I ask him to. He don't say where... I don't ask. Smoke up, man. We done got ahead of you while you was in there cleaning up. Especially this sweet little gal of yours. This must be her first pot, huh? Man, oh man. She's really turning on – ain't you, honey?" he asked, turning to face Helen.

Helen turned her smiling face to Buck's. "You know it, black daddy," she giggled, looking into his eyes as her hand moved under the table. "Ooooh," she sighed, closing her eyes in rapture. "That turns me on, too!"

"Is black gettin' more beautiful, baby? You wanna get you some of it?"

"Mmmm-hmm! I always heard black dick

was the best. You gonna prove it to me, daddy?"

"Hooo-weee, yes!" Buck yelled happily, taking Helen's face between his big hands and kissing her full on the mouth.

Danny started to get up, to protest and go around the table and jerk them apart. Then he saw Maria's sternly disapproving glare, and sat meekly back down, trembling as he sipped at his drink. His wife's mouth opened. She sucked in Buck's tongue and sighed longingly, locking her mouth to his as her cheeks hollowed in suction. Danny's glass clattered as he put it on the table.

After what seemed like an eternity to Danny, Buck pulled his thick, brown lips from Helen's puckered mouth. His big hand took hers and moved it up to her mouth, putting the half-smoked cigarette to her lips. "Suck some more pot, baby. Being high on grass makes fuckin' so much better! When you're way up there... when you come when you're way high... Lordy! Seems like it just goes on forever and ever! Makes you think you gonna die for sure and don't care even if you does! Suck it, Helen baby, suck some more stick!"

Squinting her eyes against the harsh smoke, Helen closed her lips over the soggy end of her reefer. She sucked in loud and deep, pulling the smoke directly down into her lungs.

Then she held her breath until her eyes began to water before she exhaled a tiny puff of smoke. The rest had been absorbed into her system, the desired result.

"Jew see that?" she demanded proudly of all. "I'm gettin' the hang of it. Didn't cough once! How 'bout that?"

Danny dropped his eyes as Helen brought the pot to her lips again. He heard her sucking harshly. Cursing under his breath, he picked up his own reefer and brought it to his lips.

"Allow me," a sickeningly sweet voice offered.

A lighter jumped under his nose and flashed to life. A hand moved the flame to the end of Danny's cigarette and held it there as he puffed a fire onto the end of it. He inhaled a small puff and felt like it was ripping out his lungs. When he had finished coughing, the hazy glow was already beginning to seep over him.

"Thanks," Danny said, turning to look up the arm with the lighter. Harold smiled at him, his eyes dancing with admiration.

Chapter 7

That fatuous smile. He knew he was grinning like an idiot but couldn't help it. Ridiculous,

Danny thought, bringing the roach to his lips and taking a last puff before he reached out and dropped the stick of pot, so short now that it felt hot to his fingers, into the ash tray at the centre of the table.

It was nice, though. He had to admit that the effect was pleasant. His body was so light, so buoyant. He closed his eyes. Helen's voice came to him from afar. A schoolgirl giggle. She was happy. It was good. He wanted her to be happy, just as he was.

How strange. How fantastically odd. Liquid... he was turning into liquid. It was a pleasant sensation. He sighed and let it come. The chair would no longer contain him. All the bones in his body were gone now. Somehow the fluid managed to retain a resemblance to Danny Nielsen, and clung together in a slushy whole.

With no bones to support the oozy mass his body had become, he began to slip from the chair. Like the cartoon cat who is thrown against the fence and flows liquid-like down onto the ground, Danny felt himself flowing out of the chair. How smooth, how graceful it was. Very slowly he flowed from the chair in utter contentment. His feet stopped under the centre of the table. They refused to go any further, and began to dissolve and puddle. His legs also puddled at that point and joined his now completely fluid feet.

His buttocks passed over the edge of the chair painlessly, flowed easily down onto the floor and were sucked into the puddle he was becoming. Spineless and flexible, his torso slithered snake-like out of the chair and slurped into the liquid mass on the floor. The carpet began to absorb him, his fluid self soaking into the fabric and spreading like ink dropped onto a blotter, fusing with it and becoming a stain, a permanent part of the carpet.

Panic gripped him. His head was still on the chair, balanced precariously on the edge of the seat and separated from the rest of his rapidly disappearing body. The head wanted to dive off the chair and into the fluid that was his body, to become part of the stain on Maria's carpet, to remain there forever and feel bliss again and again as Maria walked over the spot. The head floundered, could not make it, was left behind.

Groaning aloud at the unbearable separation, Danny jerked open his eyes. He blinked. He was back sitting in the chair. The others were still at the table, grinning at him, giggling. He hadn't turned to fluid at all! It had seemed so real, so real!

Looking from one face to the next, his gaze moved around the table. Maria sat beside him. Her eyes danced with evil, an awesome and beautiful thing to behold. Bess looked bored. Piss on Bess. Ellie, licking her lips and smiling at him. Lovely, Ellie, exotic Ellie. Rod, masterful and confident, with his arm around Helen's naked shoulders, his hand cupping her tit. Helen, sighing as she rubbed her neck against Rod's leather-covered arm, smiling and looking Danny in the eye. Buck, big black Buck, the jolly black giant. Helen's arm dangled across Buck. Her hand was moving in his lap. Then Harold. Fat Harold, devouring Danny with his eyes, as if he knew Danny would soon be his.

Maria got to her feet. "I think we're all in the mood to see a little exhibition now. Clear the table, Bess."

The bored expression melted from Bess' face. She jumped to her feet and picked a tray off the floor beside her chair. Moving around the table, she picked up each glass and put it on the tray. Harold's pudgy hand patted affectionately at her butt.

"Stop it, Harold!" she snapped. "I'm really not your type, am I? What's the matter? Danny got you so worked up that all rumps look alike to you?" She laughed, turning her head back to throw him a mocking look. Then she jerked her body quickly, her swaying tit splatting resoundingly into Harold's face. She picked up the tray, backing away from the table and laughing uproariously.

"Okay, Ellie," Maria said with a grin. "Feed

Helen and Danny some of that sweet chocolate box."

Her eyes gleaming in anticipation, Ellie stood and ripped off her skimpy sarong. One brown foot came onto her chair, then the other. Careful not to tip the table, Ellie placed one foot at its centre and then stepped up. Looking from first Danny to Helen, then back again, she stroked sensually at her upper thighs and lower belly. Her hand cupped over her cunt and pressed, her eyes closing for a second as she savoured the moment.

With her eyes still closed, Ellie asked, "Which one first, Maria? The Southern gentleman, or his lily-white lady?"

Fascinated, Danny watched as Ellie turned toward him and slowly sank her middle finger up into her pussy. It came back out just as slowly, glistening now with a coating of her slippery, clear fluid. Again she inserted the finger into herself, this time cooing Danny's name as it disappeared.

"The Southern gentleman's too eager," Maria chuckled. "See how he's licking his lips? Feed his lady first. Helen has never tasted cunt, have you, baby?" Maria asked, turning to see Helen's reaction.

The sight made Maria howl with glee. There sat Helen, her face clearly showing terror at the prospect of putting her mouth to the Negress' crotch. She shook her head and tried to rise. She couldn't get to her feet. Every time she got her butt off the chair, it plopped right back down. But her hands were under the table, one wrapped tightly around Rod's hard cock, the other gripping Buck, as far as possible. She could not or would not release their organs, even as Ellie knelt and stuck her cunt-slick finger into Helen's open mouth.

"Lick it clean, Scarlett," Ellie taunted, twisting and wiping her finger on Helen's tongue.

"Noo," Helen moaned, jerking her head to the side. Both her hands came from under the table and shoved at Ellie's hand.

Everyone thought it was funny. Even Danny couldn't restrain himself from joining in the loud burst of laughter.

"Hold her," Maria hissed.

Buck and Rod stifled their laughter and each took one of Helen's upper arms, sitting her firmly back down into her seat. They held her there as Maria came round the table and stopped directly behind Helen's chair.

"Pretty girl... pretty girl," Maria murmured, stroking the palm of her right hand over the back of Helen's head. "I could come to love you, Helen. I may take you away from Danny completely and let you live with Rod and me. You can sleep in the middle. We'll both make love to you every night. Would you like that, baby? Would you?"

"No!" Helen screamed. "You're insane... completely insane!"

Fingers gripped into Helen's hair and jerked her head roughly back until she was staring up at the ceiling. Maria's face came over her, a wicked smile playing at her lips.

"We'll see, baby," Maria said, "we'll see. You're made for sex. Before this party is over you'll find that out. We're gonna turn you on, doll. All the way on!"

The smile faded from Maria's mouth. Her tongue licked at her parting lips, moistening them as her face descended closer and closer to Helen's.

Unable to move anything but her legs, Helen watched wide-eyed as Maria's moist, red lips came ever closer to her mouth. The tip of her pink tongue licked nervously at her own lips. Maria meant to kiss her, Helen realised. Lust glittered in Maria's half-closed eyes as Helen looked pleadingly up into them. "No, Maria... no please don't," Helen asked timorously.

Maria ignored her pleas. She brought her lips lightly into contact with Helen's, rubbing gently from side to side, brushing Helen's lips with her own. "Yes, Helen... oh, yes, baby," she whispered, her lips flitting in a butterfly-like caress as she formed the words with her mouth against Helen's.

Then Maria could stand it no more. She groaned aloud and opened her mouth wide, covering Helen's mouth entirely with her lips. Her hand shot up and fingers pressed at Helen's chin until her mouth came open. Maria jabbed in with her tongue, tasting the sweetness of Helen's oral cavity. She licked at Helen's tongue, the walls of her cheeks, the roof of her mouth, sighing all the while and rocking her face with her eyes clamped tightly shut.

At first Helen remained passive. There was nothing she could do to prevent what was happening to her. But she didn't have to like it, and was determined to show no response whatsoever. It was perverted for one woman to kiss another like Maria was kissing her. It was wicked, unnatural. She shut her eyes to it.

The tongue kept at her, caressing her tongue and her cheeks, darting about inside her mouth, the face rocking on above her, soft and velvety. Maria's perfume caught in her nostrils as she drew in a breath. Soft lips, soft face, erotic scent, small, darting tongue that continually caressed the inside of her mouth. Perverted? Was it really? Yes. But nice... nice.

Suddenly Helen's tongue began to answer Maria's. She licked back at it, at the rough top, at the smooth, silky under surface. It was good, a sweet tongue, pleasant to the taste. A tremor passed through her body. How thrilling it was to kiss Maria! She wanted more of her... more. A guttural moan coming up from her throat, Helen formed her lips around Maria's tongue and sucked harshly. She drew it deeper into her now willing mouth, caressing it, loving it. She had it all now. The tip of her tongue played back and forth at the frenulum under the base of Maria's. The tip of Maria's tongue licked at the back of her throat. How wonderful to be kissed by Maria. As far as Helen was concerned, it could go on forever.

Then it was ending. Maria was pulling her mouth away. Helen groaned a protest as Maria's tongue slipped out of her mouth. She opened her eyes. Maria was smiling down at her. "Again," Helen pleaded. "Kiss me again."

Maria dropped her head and planted several little pecks over Helen's face. "See, baby? I know more about you than you know about yourself. I'll love you some more later. It's time for bigger and better things now."

The clutching fingers released her hair and Helen felt her head being pushed upright again. Her chair was jerked back from the table a little way. Maria's hands came to her head again, pushing it forward and down toward the table.

"Now, Ellie," Maria urged. "Feed her now."

Ellie was on her back. She scooted out till her ass hung at the edge of the table. Her feet braced beside her brown buttocks for a second, then she changed her mind and drew up her thighs against her chest.

Helen watched the dark cunt-lips relax and open as Ellie settled into a final knees-to-chest position. Red-tipped brown fingers stroked around each side of the brown ass. The fingertips hooked dark outer lips and pulled open Ellie's cunt as Helen's face was being pushed against it. For a fleeting second the inside of Ellie's cunt was visible. It was blood engorged and red-looking, just like a white woman's when she is sexually aroused. It startled Helen. Somehow she'd expected it to be black on the inside, too.

It covered her mouth and nose, feeling all warm and moist and slippery. She'd expected to get sick to her stomach with the first contact. To her surprise, Helen found it pleasant rather than sickening. Ellie's organs were not at all dirty or foul-smelling. She liked the aroma. It was a musky, womanly smell. She liked the feel of such softness covering her mouth. Her tongue went out gingerly, lapping up inside Ellie to explore the taste.

Maria pulled Helen's head away from

Ellie's cunt. Looking down into her eyes, she asked, "Well?"

"Turn me loose," Helen requested softly.

Immediately Maria let go of her head. "Hands off, boys," she told Rod and Buck. "I think Helen's ready to join the party all the way now."

The restraining male hands fell away. Helen made no effort to rise from her chair. She gazed hotly into Ellie's pussy, her hands coming up to reach out and touch it. Her left hand stroking lovingly at Ellie's up-raised thigh, she traced up and down the dark slit with the fingertips of her right. Such perfect smoothness! Ellie was every bit as delicious-feeling as Helen was herself. Often she had wished she could bend her back enough to kiss her own pussy. She'd tried, but it had proved impossible.

Now here was Ellie, beautiful from head to toe, with her pussy right in Helen's face and just begging to be kissed. It seemed so natural. Helen sighed and leaned forward. Pursing her lips and closing her eyes, she planted a tender kiss in the very centre of Ellie's lovely brown cunt. With the fingers of both hands, Helen pulled open the soft cunt lips. She stuck in her nose and inhaled. There was nothing chocolatey about Ellie's smell. It was woman scent – heady, exciting, scrumptious!

Her hands trembling with eagerness, Helen cupped Ellie's hips and moved her mouth into position. She whimpered, then opened her mouth and covered the dark pussy completely. It was the most thrilling thing Helen had ever done. Her heart beat wildly in her chest. Her pulse pounded at her temples. Not content with tasting Ellie's outer cunt alone, Helen extended her tongue slowly up the girl's vagina.

The secretions from the vaginal wells collected on Helen's taste buds. How sweet! How utterly delicious! She probed up the dark, velvety tunnel until her tongue felt chafed by the sharp edges of her lower teeth. When her taste organ could reach no further, Helen licked around and around, lapping at Ellie's insides until she had to swallow.

"Ohh, baby... baby," Ellie sighed, as Helen pulled her mouth away and swallowed the cunt juice. "That was divine!"

Looking up into Ellie's face, Helen licked at her lips and smiled. "Oh, yes," she agreed. "It was!"

"Love me some more... just like you did," Ellie urged hotly.

It was exactly what Helen had in mind. She bent her head and brought her mouth back to Ellie's saliva-wet vulva. Her tongue lashed out and eagerly licked up between the slick cunt-lips. She found Ellie's excited clitoris at the top folds of her opening and flicked it back and forth with the tip of her tongue. The inner lips came next. She licked all around the sensitive, elliptical hole, not giving a damn if what she was doing might be considered perverted or not.

"Well, Danny? What do you think of that?" Maria asked.

A grunt was his only answer. It was the most erotic sight he had ever seen. Once, on pass down in Mexico, he had seen two women make this kind of love. But they had gone about it so business-like, so matter-of-factly. But this was his wife! And she was not just pretending, she was putting her all into the lewd act. Helen was passionate as hell. Ellie, too. Both of them were totally absorbed in what they were doing, loving every minute of it!

Danny sat there trembling, watching as Helen's hands stroked the heaving brown belly. White fingers found brown tits, closed around them, squeezed urgently. Then Helen began massaging Ellie's breasts as her mouth worked incessantly down her cunt. Soon Ellie was moaning constantly and writhing about on the table, with Helen's mouth and hands following and fondling, seemingly anticipating every move.

Ellie never yelled out or announced her

orgasm, but it was plain for all to see. Her face contorted first, her eyes clamping shut and her lips drawing back over her teeth. Then her breathing turned to gasps and sighs. Her body began to tremble and tense. Then, all in one movement, her hands gripped into fists, she threw back her head and elevated her shoulders from the table, her legs flopped down around Helen's head and locked her pleasure-giving mouth tightly to her cunt, her stomach muscles began rippling spasmodically and her breathing sounded like someone dying of asthma. She shuddered and gasped at the end, then collapsed like a soggy hunk of bread.

As soon as Ellie's legs fell away from Helen's head, Maria urged her up and took her into her arms. "Turn her around and let Danny eat her before she cools down," she said to Rod, talking over Helen's shoulder. Then she hugged Helen to her and kissed her cunt-slick mouth without bothering to wipe off Ellie's juice.

Helen was ready for anything. She eagerly took Maria's probing tongue into her mouth and sucked it. It seemed so natural to put her arms around the woman and return her embrace. Their tits mashed together. The leather bra felt cool and strange as it pressed against her. But it was nice, caressing. Hazily Helen recalled Maria telling her that she loved the feel of leather on her bare skin, She'd have to try it herself. The skirt rubbed against her bare stomach. Oh yes... a leather outfit was definitely the next item on her wardrobe list!

"Trouble here," Bess called. "Danny doesn't want to eat cunt."

Maria patted Helen affectionately on the bare ass, then left and went around the table. She got two quirts out and gave one to Bess. Both women began thrashing Danny with the quirts, Maria all the while demanding that he go down on Ellie. In less than a minute he saw it her way and was hurrying to put his head between the Negress' wide-spread thighs. He went at it with gusto, licking and slurping as if it was the best tasting thing in the whole world.

"You see that he keeps at it till Ellie hollers uncle," Maria admonished Bess.

Harold came up behind Danny and stood behind his chair. The sultan's costume was now discarded. He had a tube of surgical jelly in one hand and his stiff dick in the other. He looked imploringly at Maria.

"Rod," Maria said, nodding to Harold, "you and Buck pull Ellie part way across the table. Bess, see that Danny keeps his mouth on her cunt."

Chapter 8

It was not necessary for Bess to whip Danny into following Ellie's cunt with his mouth. She did, though, and beamed down proudly at the red welts her quirt-swinging hand brought to his naked butt. So much did she enjoy beating the slobbering and whimpering Danny that she could not stop even when Ellie was in the final position. Like a madwoman she sighed and grunted as she rained blow after blow down upon Danny's vulnerable posterior.

Even Maria's sharp command telling her to quit went unheard, something that had never happened before, because she greatly feared Maria. Envied her, too. The way Maria could master the lowly male and subjugate him to her iron will had always awed Bess. She wanted that kind of power for herself, and was now lost in rapture with the illusion that finally she had it.

"Maria! She's making hamburger out of Danny's rear," Helen protested. "Stop her... please."

"Rod? Take care of it, will you, honey?" Maria asked, nodding over to Bess.

"That's enough, Bess," Rod said sternly, going around the table to take-away her quirt before Danny suffered permanent harm.

But Bess was too far gone. In her false feeling of omnipotence, she sneered at him and drew back her arm for another whack at Danny. When Rod stepped between them, preventing her blow, Bess raged and swung the quirt at him instead.

The leather thongs hit against Rod's leather shirt, sounding as if it were a very painful blow. In reality, Rod barely felt it. He merely shook his head and grabbed Bess' arm. She cursed loudly as he snatched the quirt from her hand. In frustration she tried to kick at his shins. A few of her ineffectual kicks glanced off his shins, feeling painful enough that Rod wanted no more of it.

He slapped her soundly across the face, then picked her up under one arm and carried her to the back of the room. With Bess fighting him tooth and nail, and raining a verbal torrent of abuse upon him, Rod opened the bathroom door and shoved her inside. Jerking back the shower curtain, he pitched Bess into the stall, harem-girl costume and all.

"You're out of character, Bess," he said calmly. "Playing the hell cat doesn't become you in the least. Maybe this will cool you down."

With that, he turned on the cold water full blast and laughed uproariously as Bess spluttered and pushed the hair back out of her eyes. To be sure that she stayed long enough in the shower, he sat down on the commode and laughingly shoved her back under the cold spray each time she tried to escape. Finally she was her old submissive self again, drenched and shivering and offering no resistance.

"Gonna behave yourself now?" asked Rod. When she nodded agreement, he helped her out of the soaked costume and gave her a towel. Then he went back to join the party, leaving Bess as she rubbed the water out of her hair.

Things were progressing well. As Rod came back into the orgy room, he saw that Danny was still going at Ellie's cunt. He was bent over the table now, his butt poked out and taking another kind of beating. Harold was gruntingly indulging in the activity he loved best. His pudgy hands held Danny's swaying hips as his dick plunged in and out of the previously virgin asshole.

Danny didn't seem to mind. Rod had heard him squeal once while he was inside the bathroom with Bess. But evidently that was over. The painful part now in the past, Danny appeared to have warmed to being buggered. In fact, he at times pulled his mouth from Ellie's pussy to sigh longingly and hunch back at Harold's cock. Rod shook his head. It was true. It takes all kinds to make a world.

And Helen. Sweet Helen. She now had few, if any, inhibitions left. She was on the table with Ellie, sitting on her shoulders and rubbing her pussy against Ellie's mouth. And Ellie wasn't fighting against it, either. She held Helen to her, her hands and fingers digging into Helen's buttocks and helping to rock the cunt back and forth over her mouth.

Two jobs kept Helen's hands jumping. For a few seconds she would cradle Ellie's head and press it tightly into her loins, then she would release the head and run her hands up the front of her body. Sighing deeply, Helen would then cup and fondle her own breasts, getting rougher and rougher until her fingers were twisting and burying into the soft globes. Last came her nipples, caught between thumb and forefinger, held captive for a second before Helen whimpered and pinched down on them with all her strength. Then, gasping and licking at her lips, Helen would drop her hands and clasp Ellie's head once more, pulling it harshly against her and groaning as she chanted, "Suck... suck... suck!"

Maria and Buck. Where were they? A moment later he found them, more from the sounds than from sight, in a darkened corner. Maria's leather skirt was hiked up around her waist. The bra was off entirely. Buck was the one man, other than Rod, that Maria accepted as her superior. She'd tried to dominate him once, but had wound up getting raped and loving every minute of it. Buck was too much man in every way for her to master.

He was again proving it to both their satisfaction at this minute. Maria lay on her back on the floor, with Buck on top of her and hunching his brown ass brutally down into her. Her mouth was locked to his, her fingers clawing at his back. Her wide-spread legs thrashed about and quivered each time he slammed her cunt full of thick, long, black cock.

For a moment Rod knelt beside them and watched. Seeing Buck stroke his pole in and out of Maria's twat always made his own penis rear up in readiness. It strained against the confines of his tight leather trousers, demanding relief, to be freed from its painful prison.

A flap of the same colour and texture as the rest of the leather his trousers were made from buttoned into the pants. The buttonholes were in the pants themselves, the buttons in the removable crotch covering. It was tricky to take off the crotch flap with the pants on, but Rod managed to undo the two buttons that lay between his balls and asshole. He sighed. They were the hardest ones to get undone. After they were loose, he could raise the flap and reach inside to unfasten the rest of the buttons.

As he lifted the flap, his rigid organ stood hard and proud also. Taking one of his wife's hands from Buck's back, Rod brought it to his cock and pressed her fingers around his shaft. She held it tightly and made little jerking motions as Rod unhooked the rest of his buttons. He'd intended to crawl up beside their heads and turn Maria's face to the side so he could put his cock into her mouth for a blow job while Buck finished screwing her pussy.

It was no good. Before he could act, Maria began moaning with the onset of orgasm and jerked away her hand to cup both of Buck's pistoning buttocks and help him slam his pelvis yet harder against hers. The only thing his wife could now think about was the flood of pleasure sweeping over her body. Rod didn't dare put his organ in her mouth when she was in this condition. Not any more he didn't. He still bore scars on the shaft of his dick from the one time she'd had it in her mouth while experiencing as intense an orgasm as this one promised to be.

After coming, she would be of no use to him for several minutes at the very least. The tension had been building within her since breakfast that morning. When she went, with Buck's big cock doing the sending, she'd be able to do nothing but lie there and quiver for some moments, not even knowing or caring where she was.

It was a beautiful sight to see her blow her mind like that, and to listen to the unearthly sounds she uttered while in the throes of such a soul-rending climax. It was coming now. Rod sat down beside them and watched. Maria jerked her mouth from Buck's and "Ooohed" and "Mmmmed" as her head rolled from side to side. Her eyes were shut tight to close out everything but the tide of pleasure cresting her loins. She gasped as the crest broke and flooded out through her body, going to even the tips of her fingers and toes and leaving her flesh a twitching, shuddering mass everywhere it passed.

Suddenly, she screamed out like a banshee and slapped down at the floor with the palms of her hands. The soles of her boots hit the floor at almost the same time. Feet, hands and elbows pressed down at the carpet and Buck, big and heavy as he was, was being lifted into the air atop Maria's slender and shuddering female body. Her head snapped back to support her arched position. Her lust-dazed eyes stared blankly at the near wall as she planted the top of her head into the carpet like an anchor.

Her hands left the floor and went under her body. Both elbows sank into the plush carpet as she palmed a buttock in each hand. Fingernails raked at the cheeks of her ass, bringing up painful, red welts to add to and urge the sex pleasure on to a greater peak. Feet, elbows and the top of her head: these, and Buck's bare toes, were all that remained on the floor as Maria sank her teeth into Buck's brown shoulder and hurtled over the end of the world into the personality-obliterating bliss of utter orgasmic darkness.

The unearthly sounds came pouring up from Maria's chest and throat. Some sounded like animals fighting, but not any animals that are known today. Something either out of prehistoric times or from another, and totally alien, planet. Ghostly sounds came also from deep within her, sounds so far removed from human like utterances that they would chill the blood of anyone not able to see what had caused them. Other sounds came, too, some common to a female in the shuddering depths of orgasm, some not near enough to familiar sounds to even permit description.

Then, sobbing at the end, Maria threw her arms and legs up around Buck's powerful body and collapsed, with him falling on top of her, rolling with her back and forth over the floor.

Rod left them, neither Buck nor his wife ever becoming fully aware that he'd been playing the voyeur at their expense. He felt neglected. Maria and Buck were spent for the time being. Ellie was still sucking Helen's pussy as Danny sucked hers and took Harold's prick up his ass at the same time. The ache in his organ demanded that Rod find some means of relief. Bess would soon be coming out of the bathroom, but she was less fun than jacking off. Sam was the only one that could really turn old weirdo Bess on to full steam. Bess would have to wait a while longer for that long, pointed dick. Playing the host for what he thought was a long enough period, it was now time for some sex to come Rod's way.

The one who turned him on the most was Helen. She'd been getting her cunt sucked long enough. It was now time for her to have cock, his cock. His organ standing out, his balls exposed and swaying, Rod went to the table and stopped in front of Helen. She didn't see him. Her eyes were closed and her hands were busy trying to stuff Ellie's head up into her pussy.

What a shame to bust up such uninhibited goings on, he thought. Deciding that he could wait a little longer, Rod reached out and took Helen's puckered brown nipples between his thumbs and forefingers. That she noticed.

Her eyes coming open and staring glassily at him, Helen mumbled, "W-what the h-hell?" It was many seconds later before she recognised who stood in front of her swaying body. "Rod!" she said happily, glancing down at his fingers. "Yes, darling. I'm still in your hands for the duration of the party. Do it, Rod! Do it! You know how to hurt me so good!"

Bending forward and putting their mouths together, Rod began tightening down slowly on her nipples as he drew her tongue into his oral cavity and sucked it. Soon Helen was sighing and moaning sweetly into his mouth, telling him how wonderful her tits felt at his touch. He took her to the point where she was gasping at the intensity of pain he imparted to her nipples.

"Ummmm... Oooo," she uttered, throwing back her head and gritting her teeth to keep from screaming out. "Oh God, Rod! Jesus... You're hurting me now, darling. I mean, really hurting me. Let up for a minute, will you?"

"I'm just getting started, Helen, baby," he said through a crooked smile. "When I'm finished with you, you'll know for sure whether you're a true masochist or not."

"No, Rod... no," Helen moaned, looking askance at his leering grin.

"Here it comes, baby. Brace yourself!" Rod hissed, then dug his fingers brutally into her soft nipples.

"Aargh! God! Oh my God! Aargh!"

It was unbearable. Helen stared uncomprehendingly at Rod. She'd gotten the impression that any pain would stop when it ceased to be pleasurable to her. It had seemed like an unspoken agreement between them earlier. But not now... not now!

He was killing her. Brutally, his fingers bit into her tender nipples, twisting them this way and that, pulling them out and stretching them as far as the flesh could go without tearing. She couldn't stand it another minute! Not another second! "Rod... oh shit... don't hurt me any more. Please stop... Please! I can't stand it... I can't!"

Rod relented. He liked Helen too much to ignore her pleas. As always, he found that causing pain was no thrill for him as long as the recipient did not enjoy it. Maybe he'd been mistaken about Helen. Perhaps she was not a latent masochist at all, but merely a budding hedonist who possessed the ability to enjoy all things up to their saturation points.

"Okay, sweet stuff," he said, gazing tenderly into her frantic eyes as he let go of her swollen nipples. "You win."

As her tits fell free, Helen's eyes became even more frantic. Her face screwed up in bittersweet agony. A broken sob escaped her twitching mouth.

"What's the matter, baby? What's wrong?"

"Oh, Rod! Sweet Rod!" Helen exclaimed loudly. She looked into his concerned eyes and smiled a pain-racked smile. "That was wonderful... simply marvellous."

"I thought you didn't like it."

"Me too. That's what I thought too, Rod. Then, when you so suddenly turned loose... Mmmm! It was even better going back down than it was coming up!"

"Yeah. okay, baby. I've got you pegged now. Want me to do it again?"

"No! Oh God, but they're gonna be sore as hell now."

"You can call the shots. When you say quit, I'll do it from now on."

"Really? Are you sure, Rod? You'll stop the instant I ask you to?"

"Promise."

"Well... In that case, lift me off here. There's something else I'd like to try."

Rod grinned. "Yep. Just as I thought. A budding hedonist."

"A budding what?" Helen asked, putting her arms around Rod as he lifted her from Ellie's mouth and shoulders.

"Ask me next week some time. I'm not in the mood to play dictionary right now," Rod replied, looking hotly into Helen's eyes as he stepped back from the table and let her soft body slide down his.

"Mmmm! That leather!"

"You like the feel of it on your skin?"

"And how," she said. "I'm going to get me

an outfit made from leather and wear it around the house all the time!"

"It'll lose its thrill for you if you do that. Over-exposure, too much of a good thing, you know what I mean."

"I dunno, daddy," she cooed, rubbing sensually against him. "Can you get too much of a good thing? Really?"

"Want me to pinch your tits?"

"No!"

"Get the point?"

"Okay... I get the point, all right. In fact, I think I'm getting another point," she said, opening her legs to rise on tiptoes and squeeze Rod's prick between her soft thighs.

"You want that point, baby?"

"Mmm, yes. But not right now. Oh, Rod, don't be hurt. I just damn near love you, honey. I'll take your point later, and you can be sure it'll be well taken. There's something else I want you to do to me first. That's all."

"Name it, my little hedonist," Rod said warmly.

"Be my daddy. I've been a naughty girl. Naughty girls ought to be taken over their daddy's knees and spanked."

Chapter 9

Helen let Rod take her hand and lead her over to one of the couches. She stood like a penitent child as he sat down on the edge of the cushion with his legs coming together to form a support for her to lie a cross. With her head hung and staring down at the floor, Helen shifted from one foot to the other, stealing a glance at Rod from time to time, just as she used to at her father when she was waiting for him to spank her.

"All right, Helen. Let's get it over with," Rod said, reaching out and grasping her wrist. He pulled her down across his lap, then spread his legs till one supported her lower belly and one pressed against the bottom of her breasts. "This is going to hurt me more than it is you, young lady," he said, feigning the authority of a self-righteous father, because Helen seemed to be taking the game so seriously.

"You always say that, Daddy."

"That's only because it's true. I get no pleasure from this sort of thing. I don't like to hurt my little girl, you know that. But you have to be disciplined."

"Yes, Daddy. I know I've done a bad thing. A girl my age should know better. But Tommy took advantage of me. He's older than me, you know. He's thirteen and I'm barely twelve."

"That's no excuse, Helen. Your mother and I have raised you properly. You knew it was wrong."

"Yes, Daddy. But I was curious. That's why I let him pull down my panties and touch me there."

"And did he also show you his Satan's rod?"

"Yes. It was all hard and mean-looking. He made me take it in my hand and play with it. But I wouldn't let him put it in me like he wanted to, Daddy. Honest, I didn't. His finger. That's all I let him put in me."

"For shame, child! For shame!" Rod's voice sounded ultra-condemning, but he could barely keep from laughing. Helen was into the play-acting so far that she had mentally regressed to a sexually awakening young girl. There was no doubt in his mind that the scene they were now acting out had happened to Helen, with her father playing his role, of course.

"All right, Daddy. I'm ready for you to chastise me. Drive the devils from my body and make me pure again."

"Yes, of course. It must be done," Rod said, his hand coming up and taking aim at Helen's luscious behind.

Splat! The first swat hit, catching her on

the right buttock and leaving the reddened impression of his palm and fingers.

"One devil gone," murmured Helen.

"How many devils are inside you, Helen?"

"At least a dozen, Daddy, maybe more. You'll drive them all from me, won't you? It's the only way I can be a good Christian. The devils make me do things that Christ wouldn't like."

Rod shook his head in wonder. What the hell kind of warped, religious nut was her father? "Yes, sweetheart," he soothed, going on with the game for Helen's benefit. "I'll drive all those evil devils out of my little girl. Every last one of them."

Then, counting his blows, Rod smacked his open hand down onto Helen's quivering ass eleven more times. Each time Helen hissed out a number, keeping track of the total number of devils as each was driven from her body. After the twelfth swat, Helen's rump was glowing pink all over. She whimpered and wiggled about on his lap, her side brushing hotly against Rod's erect penis.

"One more, Daddy. There's one more devil still inside me. He's the biggest one of all. Make him leave, too. Drive him out."

Drawing back his hand slowly, Rod took careful aim and whacked down at Helen's ass with great force. The smack sounded loudly through the room. It jolted Helen about on his lap, making her sob and whimper.

"Is it gone now, Helen?"

"No, Daddy. The devil's still in me. That worst one. The one that made me let Tommy touch me. He glowed when Tommy put his finger up into me."

"He's glowing now, I take it."

"More than ever, Daddy... more than ever. He's tormenting me something awful!"

Rod was puzzled. What did Helen expect of him now? What had her father done all those years ago that she wanted to relive? He decided to play it by ear. "Well... it's obvious that spanking won't drive out that tenacious devil. There must be a way to get rid of him, though."

"It helped a little when Tommy put his finger inside and wiggled it around," said Helen, her voice barely a whisper.

So that was it. The spanking had led to incest. But how far had it gone? He didn't want to ask Helen point-blank whether her father had taken her in intercourse or not. It would break the spell she was under – ruin the whole thing for her.

"Maybe if I touched you there, Helen," he mumbled.

"It might help," she whispered.

"Then I'll try it. But remember, daughter,

it's only to drive out that obstinate devil. It's for your own good."

"I won't tell Mother, Daddy. I won't tell anyone."

"Turn over, child," he said, scooting back full onto the couch.

Helen made a big issue of rubbing against his stiff dick as she turned over onto her back. Then she settled down, sighing as her eyes shut. She lay quietly. Her head and shoulders rested on the couch. Her legs were angled down with her heels pressing into the cushion, spread far enough apart to make room for his hand between her soft thighs. In that position her pelvis jutted up sharply, offering her pubis at the topmost point, then sloping down to a flat stomach.

Looking down at her, Rod could tell that she was no longer Helen the woman but had slipped back through the years completely now. She was Helen the adolescent girl, lying on her father's lap in a highly agitated state. Her expression was both fearful and at the same time expectant. The heat from her freshly spanked bottom warmed his thighs as she softened around them. Her hip pressed unconcernedly against his hard dick. The sound of her breathing, the rise and fall of her belly and breasts, belied the calm composure she pretended.

"Here, Helen? Is this where Tommy touched you?" asked Rod, his fingertips pressing lightly at her cunt.

"Yes, Daddy, that's where. Are you going to put your finger in it like Tommy did?"

"Of course. If Tommy's finger sent the devil on the run, mine should drive him out entirely, because it's bigger," Rod told her, inserting his middle finger slowly up into her warm vagina. "There," he said, stopping when his palm came against her vulva. "Is he gone yet?"

"He's dodging, Daddy. Maybe you'd hit him if you wiggled up inside me."

Knowing what she wanted, Rod massaged the walls of her vagina gently and thoroughly. Little by little Helen began moaning and twisting about on his lap. "It isn't helping, is it?" he asked in all seriousness.

"It's only making him madder, Daddy. He's gone and built a fire up inside of me. It's getting hotter and hotter. I don't think I can stand it much longer."

"You won't suffer the heat much longer, Helen. That devil is surely a mean one. But don't you worry over it. I know how to take care of him. Your mother has the same trouble from time to time. I can always drive the devil from her, and I can do it for you, too."

"How, Daddy? How?"

Rod picked her up in his arms and stood,

then turned and laid her on the couch. He put one of her legs up over the back of the couch, then pushed her other leg off and placed her foot on the floor. Taking his pulsing cock in his hand, he knelt between her legs. "I've got a devil-stick, too. I'll drive him out with it."

"But yours is so big, Daddy. I'm afraid it'll hurt me."

"Only for a moment," he assured, coming on top of her and working the head of his dick into the softness of her damp pussy.

Then, to give her the effect of first intercourse, Rod hunched forward with all his might, hitting into her and planting his cock up into her belly to the very hilt.

"Oohhh... *Oh, Daddy*!" Helen screamed out shrilly, shutting her eyes and making a face of intense pain. She began moaning and whimpering, complaining that it was killing her.

"It's the devil fighting for his life," Rod grunted, stroking rhythmically in and out of her cunt. "Help me slay him, Helen. The pain will stop as soon as he's dead, I promise."

Moaning assent, Helen threw her arms around him and began hunching up her cunt to meet his powerful thrusts. Seconds later she breathlessly informed him that he was right. "The devil's dead. He's dead. The pain is gone," she gasped brokenly. "But the fire... it's burning even hotter than before! I can't stand it, Daddy... I can't!"

"Don't give up, baby. Keep fighting," he hissed. "We'll win over evil together. Stamp out the fire, Helen. Help me stamp it out."

Helen threw her legs up around his ass and stamped for all she was worth, her heels banging into his pistoning butt as if her very life depended on it. Soon she was wailing and sobbing through a climax as he kept pumping his cock forcefully in and out of her fluttering vagina. "Now, Daddy, now," she screamed. "Pee on the fire and put it all the way out!"

Himself straining for orgasm, Rod was pushed over the brink by Helen's deliciously dancing vagina and her urgent plea for him to extinguish the last flames of her dying fire. His balls drew up tight against his body in readiness. The head of his cock began to twitch out of control deep within Helen's clasping pussy. Then, slamming his pubic mound roughly against hers, groaning and grunting, Rod held in all the way and squirted jet after jet of hot come over the mouth of Helen's twitching womb.

A tremor swept over Helen each time a squirt of his come shot up inside her. She whimpered throughout his orgasm, holding him tightly to her and sighing softly, "It's out... it's out... The fire's out."

They lay locked together for perhaps five minutes longer, then Rod withdrew his limber rod and sat up, reaching for a box of tissues and taking two for himself before he passed the box on to Helen. Both cleaned themselves, then went hand in hand to join the others, who were now gathered back around the table, sipping another drink and puffing another stick of pot.

"Really, Rod," Maria chided. "I've always known you were a man of many talents, but it came as a complete surprise to me that you were a holy man. Exorcising devils! That's just too much," and she began to laugh hysterically, the others joining her sudden, outburst.

Helen's cheeks flushed. She dropped her head to avoid their leering faces. They all knew her secret now, even Danny. Danny knowing was the worst of all, the most humiliating. What would he think the next times he kissed her father on the cheek? It had only happened that one time, but would Danny believe that? Could she even face her father with Danny there after this! She began to sob, crying big, hot tears that scalded her cheeks.

"Oh, baby... baby," Maria soothed, rushing to take Helen into her arms. She apologised profusely, insisting time and again that no one thought anything of it.

Because she wanted to, because she needed to, Helen accepted Maria's apology.

She forced herself to smile and allowed Maria to lead her to an empty seat between Danny and Buck. She preferred not to sit with Buck on the one side of her and her husband on the other, but it was the only available chair, so she quietly settled into it and began sipping at her waiting drink.

Brown fingers closed around one of her naked thighs while Danny eagerly stroked his palm up the inside of her leg nearest him. The brown hand patted her reassuringly, then moved up to the table and put the handmade cigarette to her lips. A lighter snapped. Helen moved her face till the tip of the grass was in the flame, then puffed deeply.

"When are you gonna bring Sam?" Bess wanted to know, her voice on edge and near whining. She looked a mess. No make-up, hair straight and stringy, with breasts sagging now that she was naked and hunched over the table.

Danny's fingers moved excitedly over Helen's just-fucked pussy. He couldn't keep his hands off her. It was true, just as he'd always suspected. Helen was not a virgin on their wedding night. He now knew that it was her own father who burst the cherry that was by all rights his, Danny's, her husband's. And just now, watching Rod play her father and re-enact the lewd episode on the nearby couch, he'd almost flipped his wig, and thought for sure his cock would spew forth a spray of come without ever being touched.

"Everybody's had their fun but me," Bess complained. "Go get Sam. I want Sam."

"You'd better go get him, Rod. Let Bess have her kicks," Maria said. "Maybe watching it will snap the rest of us back into shape."

"Come with me, Buck," Rod urged, and when Buck got to his feet, both men walked over to the door. Rod reached up and picked the key from its resting place over the top frame, then unlocked the door and out they went, Rod with his dick and balls swaying through the hole in his leather pants, and Buck right behind him, bare-assed naked.

Ellie, Harold and Maria sat listening as Bess rattled happily on about how much she'd been looking forward to her romp with Sam. The woman could hardly sit still, so eager was she to copulate once again with her "absolute favourite lover of all time." She talked incessantly, the others egging her on and enjoying the obvious impatience she displayed.

"Look," Bess urged, standing up on the seat of her chair and pulling open her cunt lips. "Just thinking about Sam makes me drool like that."

Though he tried to hide it, Danny was every bit as excited as Bess. He was curious about this mysterious Sam who was waiting till

Maria okayed his joining the party, but other and more personal images loomed larger inside his mind. His fingers were slipping rapidly in and out of Helen's cunt under the table, three of them! After her session with Rod, it had been easy to work those three fingers up into her. Her cunt was stretched and loose, just as it had been that night when Rod first screwed her. Its present condition thrilled Danny.

He brought his mouth to Helen's and kissed her. She sighed and took his offered tongue into her mouth, licking and sucking at it as his fingers kept working at her slippery pussy. Then she pushed him away and took another drag from her reefer.

"Helen? Honey?"

"What is it, Danny?" she asked, without bothering to look his way. Forming her lips to the wet end of the reefer, she again sucked harshly, drawing the biting smoke deep down into her lungs.

"We haven't had a chance to talk all evening."

"So?" she said, then exhaled a tiny puff of unabsorbed smoke.

"So," he said, fumbling for words. "Are you having a good time?" It was such a stupid thing to ask, under the circumstances. Immediately he regretted having said it.

"Yeah... I guess so. I don't think you could

really call this wingding a party, not by my definition of the word, but I'm getting turned on pretty good. That's what you wanted, wasn't it?"

"Don't, Helen. I didn't know it would be like this."

"'Don't Helen', shit. After what I saw you doing, don't tell me to don't. How did it feel up your ass, Danny? Looked like you enjoyed the hell out of it. In fact, it turned you on so much that I may try it myself."

A crimson flush creeping over his cheeks, Danny averted his eyes. "What about Buck?" he asked shortly.

"What about him?"

"Well... the way you were acting earlier, I kind of got the impression..." he stopped, unable to complete the thought in words.

Helen turned toward Danny and gazed inquiringly into his eyes. The question in her mind was never asked. The answer was obvious in Danny's expression. The way his upper lip twitched out of control gave the first hint. And his eyes, so tortured yet imploring, begging her to say it. She broke into a warm smile and reached for his loins under the table. There was no doubt about what Danny wanted. His prick was as hard as a rock.

"Why, Danny," she teased. "Really? Do you really want me to?"

His mouth opened to answer, but no words came out. He wanted badly to tell her what was on his mind but could not.

"That's rich," she laughed. "That's really rich!" Dropping his gaze from her face, Danny made himself busy with his drink.

His hand shook as he brought the glass to his mouth. Tilting it too suddenly and too far, some of the drink ran down and dribbled off his chin.

"My God," Helen exclaimed. "If just thinking about it does all that to you, maybe I shouldn't. You might have a heart attack and die on the spot."

"Hey," Maria called. "What you two got going? Let the rest of us in on it."

"Not on your life," Helen shot back, grinning. "If I tell you, then my husband will know for sure, and I don't want that. I'd rather keep him in suspense."

"That's a no-no. We don't keep any secrets from each oth–"

The door burst open without warning, and in came Buck, grinning from ear to ear. "Spread 'em, Bess. Your lover has arrived," he announced.

Rod wheeled the strange contraption through the door.

"Sam! You beautiful creature, you. Come to mama," Bess said excitedly, jumping to her feet, and, turning around, dramatically thrust her backside towards the weird mess of wheels, pistons, wires and spokes that sat atop something that looked like a hospital gurney or the sort of utilitarian trolley for hot drinks in a factory.

Rod reached down and made some last minute adjustments to the device. The Sexual Arousal Machine – S.A.M. for short – was his invention, and, powered by electricity, its lethal, unremitting stamina was legendary. It could fuck anything to a standstill. Sexual Agony Machine might have been a better term for it.

"Baby, baby," Bess cooed. "Did you miss me? Did you miss Bess the way Bess missed you?"

Rod switched on Sam. There was a low hum and the flywheel started to rotate, faster and faster. An awesome flesh-coloured rubber dildo propelled back and forth, waggling aggressively, while a tiny stream of lubricant dripped down onto it from a spigot, causing it to glisten obscenely. Bess moved over so that she could straddle the thrusting phallus. She clenched her hands into fists and just stood there, quivering slightly, as the big rubber rod hummed and plunged between her thighs, slicing through the groove of her cunt for well over a minute. She "Oohed" and "Ahhed" softly, unashamedly responding to Sam's flashing manhood in full view of the others. Then, little by little, she began backing toward a couch, verbally coaxing Sam to follow as Rod wheeled the fucking machine after her.

"That's it, Sam. Come on, Sam. Mmmm... boy... good boy. Follow mama all the way. All the way."

Danny stared bug-eyed at the strange pairing of robot and woman, but Helen seemed somewhat repulsed by the way Bess carried on over the machine.

"So that's Sam," Helen remarked. "That's what Bess has been hollering for all evening? A damned vibrator!"

"You ever tried it?" Maria countered.

"Ugh! I prefer the real thing."

"Sam's got the longest, slimmest, hottest, slickest dick you ever saw, baby. I don't go for him like Bess does," Ellie broke in. "But it's kinda nice for a change. After his true love gets done with him, I might get on my hands and knees tonight – Sam's always ready and willing, always able to get it up. Rod rigged up a belt, too, so you can be strapped in there – no mercy shown! I was tied up to Sam for nearly an hour once. Damn near killed me, but I came so many times I lost count... Mmm! But that's not the best part, not by a long shot. You want to know how Sam comes?"

Helen shook her head. Ellie's defence of woman-machine intercourse surprised her. Ellie was so clean, so neat. It was hard to believe she would want to do it with a messy, oily machine that squirted out some sort of disgusting, synthetic gunk.

"Well," said Ellie, putting down her drink but not taking her eyes off Bess and Sam. "When Rod flicks one of those switches, Sam blasts his 'come' right up into your vagina. I mean, it's like the most incredible sensation in the world."

"You're puttin' me on," Helen accused.

"No, baby, no. Have you ever felt a guy come inside your pussy? You may think you have, but I doubt it, really. This, on the other hand, is for real. You really feel that stuff squirting up inside you."

Helen recalled that she had never really felt a man squirting semen up her. Sensed it, imagined it, perhaps. She squinted her eyes and nodded at Ellie. "Yeah, since you mention it, I think you're right. I don't think I ever did."

"And another thing it can do. Sam can be inflated, just like a dog's knot."

"A dog's knot?"

"A male dog's dick has that knot puffed out on it, so he can't pull it out of the female."

"That's terrible!"

"No, it's not. That's the way they come.

Their juice doesn't squirt out like a man's does. The juice is what makes the knot come on the dog's prick. It's nature's way of making sure that the female conceives. They keep trying to pull apart, and little by little the come drains out and the knot disappears. It's simple, really."

"I don't wanna be hung up like I was with some damned dog," Helen said emphatically.

"Doesn't work that way in a woman's vagina. Too loose to hold the knot like that. Feels great, though, like a small balloon swelling up inside you. Shit. I better shut up or I'll talk myself into it," Ellie moaned, as if it was getting too personal and exciting for her to talk about. "Just watch Bess and see if it doesn't look good to you."

"I just can't believe it," Helen insisted. "I've heard about this kind of thing going on, but I thought it was a figment of some crackpot's imagination."

"Hush, Helen," Maria told her authoritatively. "If it bugs you so much, don't watch. But the rest of us want to see and hear the show."

Buck was sitting beside Helen again. He took her hand and put it on his cock, pressing her fingers around his thick shaft. Leaning his mouth up close to her ear, he whispered, "Feel that, baby. Feel good to you?"

Helen looked quickly up into his face. The gleam in his eyes told her the time was drawing near. She shuddered and nodded her head.

"You watch that gizmo hump Bess all you want to," he told her in a soft voice. "But don't get no ideas about you taking seconds. The next cock goin' in you is gonna be mine."

It had been working around to this all evening. Helen had known Buck would have her before the party was over from the moment she walked in the door and saw him dancing with Bess. For a while, earlier, when she'd first gotten high on grass, the thought of his monster prick pushing up into her cunt had been appealing. But now? Now it was going to happen. It was no longer merely a thought. A frustrating mixture of fear and anticipation swept over her body, leaving shivers and cold sweat in its wake.

Chapter 10

The weird scene on the couch grew progressively hotter and hotter. Bess' hands hovered above the machine's flashing piston, trembling and jerking, with fingers outstretched and spread. It was plain that she wanted to touch her 'lover', to caress its head and to sink down further onto the shaft that shot between the groove of her wide-spread cunt. The pink phallus flashed out like a spear, prodding deeply into her slit, staying embedded and jabbing at the weeping walls of her vagina.

"Christ... oh Christ," longingly.

Sam's action was relentless: he kept at her, the long rubbery tool sometimes, almost by chance, hitting the depths of her cunt, sometimes just grazing her asshole or oil-drenched outer cunt. It was getting too good for Bess to endure much longer. A constant stream of sighs, groans and moans issued forth from her open mouth as her body writhed about in its slumped position on the couch.

"Sam... Sam... darling Sam," Bess wailed, contorting herself to reach down and take the mechanical peter into her eager hand; as her fingers gripped around it, Sam fucked her hand mindlessly, automatically.

"No, darling," Bess protested, jerking away her hand and slapping the couch where she wanted to be fucked in more comfort, "over here. Let's do it on the couch!" Bess crawled up onto the couch and assumed a knees-to-chest position, offering her vulnerable ass to the relentless machine as she laid her head down on a cushion and grinned toward the table of onlookers.

"Get it, boy. Come on, Sam. Get it," Bess

coaxed, in a voice quavering with lust. She reached back between her parted legs and fingered open her cunt. "There, Sam. Fuck it, boy. Fuck it."

Sam, of course, needed no other encouragement. The rasping command brought his controller into action, wheeling the gurney towards the couch; the play was quite familiar to Rod, and even though he'd taken part many times, he was eager to play his role again. Bess had called out his cue, and he took it confidently from there on.

With the gurney in position, wheels locked down, Sam took his place between Bess' protruding feet. Rod could see down into her held-apart red cunt and then he adjusted the speed control and manoeuvred the now slowly thrusting artificial penis so that it was nudging her genitals.

"Baby... oh, baby," Bess moaned, her fingers encircling and guiding the big, slick organ into her seething pussy.

Turning up the speed dial, Rod made Sam drive the full length of his long, slim penis into Bess. Then, taking the leather harness, he strapped it tightly around Bess' torso and turned the speed and thrust dials to their maximum. If Bess felt any pain from his new tempo, she didn't show it. Her hand flattened over the bottom part of her stomach and moved till her middle finger was busily flicking her clitoris back and forth. The fingers on her other hand, resting on the couch above her head, clenched down into a fist so tight that her knuckles turned white. Bess heaved a sigh of deep satisfaction and dreamily closed her eyes.

Helen's voice burst forth in a hoarse whisper, "Good Lord!"

"What's the matter, baby?" asked Maria, grinning. "Gettin' to ya?"

"That's the dirtiest thing I ever saw," she said, then added in a faint whisper, "but damn... is it ever exciting!"

"Wanna try it?"

"Oh no, Maria! I couldn't let myself into that kind of thing."

"Some afternoon?" Maria coaxed. "Just you and me and Sam?"

Helen quickly glanced around to see if any of the others were looking at her. When she was sure all eyes but hers and Maria's were staring at Sam and Bess, she turned back to Maria, looking hungrily into her smiling eyes as she furtively nodded her head.

On the couch, Sam's frenzied tempo and long, stabbing thrusts were creating wet, sloshing sounds as he drove his cock in and out of her pussy. The demonic machine was operating at incredible speeds, pistoning back and forth so fast that it was impossible to tell where it was at any particular point. A fast-shuttered camera might have been able to catch the pink rubber dildo in one spot, but not the human eye. It was a frantic, lightning swift motion, a blur of movement.

Bess was nearly out of her mind. An incoherent jumble of sounds poured from her mouth. She whimpered and cried, then laughed shrilly and rubbed her face back and forth into the cushion. Both hands now at her head, she alternated between pulling her hair and slapping the couch, like a wrestler pinned to the mat and suffering greatly.

Then she froze, her mouth and eyes wide open and staring out blankly into the room. "Oh god!... *Oh god*!" she yelled, and began trembling from head to toe.

Panting like a steam engine straining up the side of Pike's Peak, Bess shuddered uncontrollably through a long, drawn-out orgasm of unbelievable intensity. Finally, at the end, her eyeballs rolling about in their sockets, and moaning as if she were dying, Bess slumped forward onto the couch, trying to break her union with the fucking robot's long, skinny dick. Finally Rod took pity and unbuckled the leather harness that held her so tightly in place.

"Oh Lordy!" It was Ellie, on her feet and hurrying over to the couch. In a frenzy of lust, she hooked her hands behind Bess and rolled her off the couch. Before Bess thudded to the floor, Ellie leaped on the couch and took her place, kneeling and pushing her ass back at Sam. "Hurry, Rod... hurry. Make Sam do his thing," Ellie hissed.

There were no preliminaries this time, no. Neither woman nor, of course, machine needed them. One was raging with lust, with raw animal need. The other was totally devoid of any emotion. Ellie's human intelligence was for the moment lost to her, a superficial thing that had buckled under the more basic and universal strength of the urge for sexual fulfilment. The sounds she made as she backed on to Sam and rammed his hot cock deep into her belly were pre-human in origin, animalistic snarls and grunts. The machine appeared positively civilised by comparison.

"Look at 'em go! Jesus... look at 'em! " Buck shouted.

His thick cock stood hard and black, weeping clear fluid from the pouting mouth at the tip of his glans. Boom, boom, boom went his heart, pumping the blood out through his massive body at a frenzied rate. With each beat of his heart the big penis jerked and swayed, demanding and drawing his attention to his burning need for copulation. "Now," he hissed, "now!" and jumped to his feet, catching the chair as he rose and flinging it to bounce off the wall behind him. He turned toward Helen, his cock slapping her in the face with a splat.

Helen stared at the sturdy, black cock, at the heavy bag of swaying balls between his legs. The lewd scene with the machine had set her loins burning hotter than they ever had in her life. Her nostrils were flared, her breathing laboured. With a guttural groan she reached out for Buck's ebony genitals. One small, white hand cupped his nuts and rolled them about as the other gripped the base of his organ and held it still. She rubbed her cheek against the bulging head of Buck's cock, then moaned and opened her mouth wide to take the next inevitable step.

Danny saw it all. His wife, panting and eager, willingly bending forward and kissing the black cock she gripped so lightly. He felt light-headed, and feared that at any moment he might faint away. It was horrible to see Helen kissing and licking at that black guy's dick. The sight was pure torture for Danny. Helen was wild for it, that was plain for all to see. But the worst part was not Helen's reaction. It was his. Danny thrilled at his wife wanting Buck. She was going to screw the black man. Danny knew there was nothing he could do to stop it happening.

But he didn't want to stop it. Had he held a

gun in his hand he still would not have tried to stop it. His mind reeled, shouting, "Fuck her, fuck her, fuck her," inside his head. He wanted to watch it, to see the expression on his wife's face as that huge, black cock spread her cunt more than it had ever been spread before and disappeared up into her white belly. He didn't have long to wait.

Helen had the head of Buck's dick in her mouth and was licking and sucking loudly. Her eyes were shut, her cheeks hollowed. Her expression said that what she was doing thrilled the hell out of her inhibited, lily-white Southern mind. She slurped wetly as Buck shoved away her mouth.

"Let's fuck," Buck said, reaching out and picking her up with his hands under her armpits. He lifted her from the chair like a child, and raised her up till her eyes looked down at him. "You ready, baby?"

Helen's eyes devoured him. "Yes," she whispered. Then her legs went out and clamped around his body, pulling her crotch up against his chest. Her ankles locked at the small of his back, her toes curling under and her heels pressing into his buttocks. "Shit yes, daddy. Give it to me! Give me that big, black cock! Lower me down and impale me with it!"

Buck grinned up at Helen, lowering her slowly and letting her wet cunt catch and jerk along his chest and stomach. Finally he felt the warmth of her cunt pressing over the head of his dick. He stopped there, holding the trembling white girl still, savouring the tight fit of her outer lips around his glans.

"Go on," she urged Buck. "Let me down over it!"

"Helen, you silly little honky. Don't you know this is gonna ruin you for white cock for the rest of your life? After I get through with you, that husband of yours won't be able to touch either side of your pussy with that little peter of his."

"I don't care, Buck," Helen moaned. "Fuck me. I've got to have it right now!"

"You gonna have it, baby... stuck clear up to your tits!" Buck grunted, suddenly releasing her to lower herself down onto his cock.

She sank down only a fraction of an inch, wincing in pain and throwing her arms about his neck. "Oh God... Buck? It's too big for me! It won't go in... it hurts!"

"Relax your legs. You got it all tensed up." He cupped the cheeks of her ass. "Let loose your legs. I got you now, you won't fall."

Fearfully, she did as he said, unlocking her ankles and letting her calves slide down the backs of his legs. Her pussy relaxed and took in half of his massive organ. Helen's breath sucked in harshly, and she stopped her descent by clamping her heels on the insides of his calves. She gaped wild-eyed at him, her mouth hanging open and gasping for air, her tits jiggling and swaying as they rose and fell rapidly.

"Good so far?"

"Yesss... Christ, yes!"

"Git the rest of it, baby. It's the best part!"

Little by little, Helen gingerly let herself down around Buck's black stanchion, sighing and moaning as her face mirrored the pure delight of being filled so thoroughly.

"Oh, Buck... darling man!"

"A little more, baby. There's a little more. Take it all."

Though she doubted it would be possible, since the head of his cock was already nudging her womb, Helen licked her lips and nodded, then closed her eyes and eased down against the hot knob. Nothing happened for a second. Then, very slowly, her uterus began to give way, slipping further up into her body and elongating her vagina to take the rest of Buck's prick inside.

She shuddered and cried out, "Oh... oh... oh," over and over.

"Is it hurtin' you too much, Helen?" Buck asked.

She wouldn't answer until the lips of her cunt were pressing into the coarse hair surrounding the base of his cock. Then she groaned mournfully and rocked back, keeping only their loins together as her upper body angled out away from his. She opened her eyes and smiled up at his face, holding on with her hands clasped behind his neck. "It doesn't hurt... not now. Oh Lord, Buck. I never knew... never knew."

"What's that?" Buck asked, not really giving a damn now that she had the full length of his organ up inside her warm belly.

"Like this... I never knew it could be this good. What a man... what a wonderful man!"

Buck let go of her ass and let her hang. He walked around the table with her like that for the others' voyeuristic benefit, then sat down on the floor and lay back, leaving Helen sitting astride his loins with his cock planted to the hilt up inside her heaving belly. "Go at it, baby. Nothin' gives me greater pleasure than to see a white Southern wife bouncing her ass up and down on my cock right before her husband's eyes."

"Danny doesn't mind," she said sultrily, glancing over to the table and catching his eye. "He's been waiting all evening to see this. Haven't you, darling?" she asked, gazing brazenly into her husband's eyes.

"Don't be so cruel," Buck said mirthfully. "You're gettin' more and more like Maria."

"Come over here, Danny," Helen ordered, ignoring Buck's remark and beginning to move her cunt up and down over his big cock. "I want you to get a good look. Come on!"

Danny pushed back his chair and got tremblingly to his feet, then walked over and stood beside them.

"You've got a hard-on, Danny," Helen said, grinning as she raised herself a little higher and then sank slowly back down till the black dick was once more gone from sight.

Danny shifted uneasily, looking down at his dick as if to see if his wife's accusation was accurate.

"Watch us, Danny. Look at it," Helen urged hotly.

Danny lowered his eyes. Buck's big cock could not be seen at all. Helen's pussy had it all. Their pubic hair was all he could see of either of their genitals. Sex-wet pubic hair, curly and coarse and tangled together where they joined. Then Helen began to rise very slowly, sighing as she exposed more and more of the slick, glistening black cock for Danny to look at. And he looked. He couldn't tear his eyes away. Up she came, until at least six inches of black pole showed between their loins. His wife's cunt-lips were distended tautly around the thick shaft, as if her pussy was sucking reluctantly at the loss, fighting to retain the monster cock within her body. Her clinging cunt-lips climbed higher up the pole. The crown at the back of the swollen glans came suddenly into view.

Hesitating there undecidedly, Helen studied Danny's face. His expression was one of pure agony. She smiled the same evil smile she'd seen Maria flash earlier in the evening, knowing that Danny both hated and loved the sight she was presenting him with. The knowledge spurred her on. Something deep within her longed to cause Danny discomfort, to humiliate him in front of the others, to degrade and dominate him. She twitched her cunt around Buck's glans, then tightened down and expelled it from her as she raised on up to her knees.

"Squat down and get your face up close, honey. Take a good look at me."

As if it were the natural thing for him to obey, Danny squatted beside them and leaned over Buck, bracing himself on the far side of Buck's hips and moving his face up close to Helen's pussy. His face contorted. He groaned aloud at the sight. His wife's cunt-lips were puffy and swollen, parting and standing wide open. Her smaller inner lips were also swollen, and coloured a fiery red with passion. He gawked up into her gaping hole and whimpered.

"Is that the way you like to see it, darling?" Helen asked sweetly.

Danny nodded dumbly, still looking hotly up into her cunt.

"You want to kiss it? Come on, Danny, and stick your tongue up in it, Helen taunted, undulating her hips up to his mouth.

Danny backed away and looked up into her face. His eyes pleaded for her to give up the sadistic game.

"If you don't kiss it, I may have to quit fucking Buck. I don't feel right about it. Maybe if you took his cock in your hand and gave it to me..."

Automatically his hand went out and grasped the thick black cock, bending it toward Helen's pussy.

"That's nice, Danny. It makes me feel better about the whole thing, just to know you approve. There's one more thing, though... Buck's dick and my pussy should be married to make it really okay. In fact, I insist on it. You can perform the ceremony for us, darling."

Danny didn't understand what she wanted. He looked up questioningly into his wife's face.

"Give us your blessing, darling. Kiss my cunt."

Though he knew Helen was making a fool of him, Danny couldn't resist doing as she asked. He bent his head and brought his mouth up to her yawning cunt, pursing his lips and pressing them into her warm opening. The urge to lick up inside her, where the black cock had been, was too strong. His tongue shot up into her vagina and licked in a circle. Then he groaned and pulled his mouth away.

"Yes. Now give Buck your blessing. Kiss the head of his penis." Danny stared up at her grinning face. She meant it! He turned to face the black cock and stopped, shaking his head in refusal. That was too much. He would not do it. Hands pressed suddenly at the back of his head, pushing his open mouth down around Buck's big glans. His tongue swept twice around the warm, velvety head of Buck's dick before he thought to jerk free. The taste of cock lingered hauntingly on his tongue as Danny resumed his squatting position beside his wife and her black stud.

"Now, Danny. You watch, honey. Watch close, 'cause I'm gonna give this lovely black stallion the wildest ride you ever saw," Helen cooed.

And she began to make good her promise. Smiling at her husband and looking him in the eye, Helen reached under her pelvis and took Buck's cock. Gripping it with both hands, one at the base and the other far enough above to leave a band of black showing between her white hands, Helen descended with a sigh, and formed her cunt-lips over the bulging black glans. She hovered there, with only part of the cock's head embedded within her tautly stretched lips.

The twitching of Danny's lower lip and the pained expression that came over his staring face excited Helen. She teased him by moaning and rolling her hips about, bending Buck's penis around in a little circular motion. Pulling almost out of contact, she caressed the tip and watched Danny's face as her cunt-lips slid up and down over the black glans.

Danny couldn't stand it. Groaning, he leaned over and brought his mouth to Helen's pussy, kissing and licking both her soft cunt and the hard head of Buck's organ. His tongue darted rapidly about, tracing around the cock head as it followed the elliptical cunt. It worked between them and flicked at the eye of Buck's dick, with Helen's inner lips pressing warmly from the other side.

Then the cock was moving away. For a second Danny was torn by indecision. He wanted to kiss them both at the same time, as they touched together. Now that was impossible. Helen was pushing the black cock up toward Buck's abdomen, taking it away from him, teasing him. Planting a quick kiss on his wife's cunt, Danny followed the cock like it was a powerful magnet. Without hesitation he placed his hands over Helen's and pulled the dick back upright. His mouth opened and took in the exposed portion, letting the hot black head snuggle into the tissue at the back of his throat as his lips pressed against Helen's hand.

She watched it for a moment, licking her lips as her husband sucked Buck's dick. Then she took his face in her hands and pulled him up. He looked so guilty – like a little boy caught doing something wrong.

"Helen? Helen, I ..."

"It's all right, darling," she whispered, and kissed him.

He smiled weakly, then backed away to his squatting position to see the action at close range.

Buck was impatient as hell. "Come on, baby, get with it. I thought you wanted to fuck. Looks like the most important thing to you is puttin' on a good show for hubby."

"I want him to see it. It excites him."

"Good! Then hop on and show him what it's all about. I'm excited pretty much, myself. If you don't put that tight little cunt around my dong right this minute, I'm gonna throw you on your back and give it to you rough as hell."

"Later, tiger. I'll tell you when," Helen said, smiling as she took his dick in one hand and brought it to her cunt. "Mmm," she sighed, wiggling down over the swollen head. Then she stopped, looking down into Buck's eyes and grinning. "You ready?"

"Ready and wai-uh, uhh, oouu! Yes, baby... oh yes!!"

Helen had dropped suddenly, taking the entire pole up into her tight vagina with one shuddering downward plunge. Her thighs and buttocks hit down onto Buck so hard the splat could be heard clear across the room. She perched there now, her hands clenched into fists and raised on either side of her head. Mouth hanging open and gasping for breath, she rocked to and fro, bending Buck's stony rod at the base and feeling its head massage deep inside her guts.

It was good – so good! Never had she enjoyed such a deep and satisfying penetration. She sobbed aloud, clamped the walls of her vagina tightly around the thick shaft, and fell forward to press her mouth to Buck's. Those thick lips so warm, so soft, so pleasantly accepting her red lips and returning her passionate kiss.

"Mmm," she moaned into his mouth. "Oh, Buck... daddy... daddy."

She'd intended to tell him how wonderful his big, hot dick felt as it pushed the top end of her vagina up into her belly and lengthened her to fit him. It was marvellous how that had made her feel. She wanted to tell him about it, to let him know what a thrill it had been for her. She was even thinking of declaring that she loved him, for at that moment she did. No man, not Danny or her father, either, had ever given her the utter bliss that Buck just had. How could she help but love such a magnificent man?

But he had stopped her words, very deliciously, very suddenly, by thrusting his tongue into her open mouth. She'd accepted it gratefully, mewling and licking at it and sucking and trying to pull it down into her stomach and make it meet the head of his pleasure-giving cock. His tongue in her mouth, stuck so far back that its tip licked down into her throat, his penis in her cunt, stuck so far up that it felt like the head was caressing the insides of her tits – bliss, pure and unadulterated! Two of his organs in her, one at either end of her body, both hot and moving and stroking at her, and feeling so goddamned good that Helen never wanted it to stop, never! Once again she tried to swallow his tongue and suck up his cock until they met and welded together at her very centre, thereby fixing him within her for all time to come, joining their two bodies together inseparably.

It wouldn't work. She wailed a protest into his mouth at the callous injustice of it all, then pulled her mouth away and began riding him at a gallop, with the palms of her hands pressing on his chest and her tits swaying frantically above him.

"Hoo, uh, oh," she chanted hoarsely, staring down at his face and pumping her hips up and down over his loins for all she was worth. "Sweet man... sweet dick... big, hot, sweet dick," she groaned out loud, stopping suddenly and grinding her cunt down forcefully to savour the pulsing head in the depths of her guts.

She gritted her teeth and moaned, closing her eyes and lifting her hands from his chest to rear back on his cock. Little by little she reared further back, angling her body down above his legs.

"Oh God," Helen whimpered. "Oh God!"

Stopping all intentional movement, Helen hung like that, with her head slumped and rolling back and forth on her shoulders. Her hands shot up and squeezed brutally into her soft tits. Her toes pulled down and curled against the bottoms of her feet. A sudden tremor swept over her entire being, making her body appear to jerk. She gasped, then began shuddering and sobbing brokenly, wailing out her orgasm in the vilest of gutter language.

When her climax receded, Helen heaved a deep sigh and broke into a smile, looking upside down at the wall behind her.

"Buck? You still there, daddy?" she called.

"Can't you feel me?" he asked, his voice tinkling with laughter.

Breaking into a giggly laugh, Helen let her body slump down more and braced herself with the top of her head touching the floor. "Shit, man. I'm dead below the waist. Can't feel a thing down that way."

"Well I do!" he moaned. "Goddamn you, woman. Sit up. You're about to break my cock off inside you!"

She laughed again. "Mmmm! That'd be nice. Walking around like that ought to keep me coming all day!"

"Cut'ta shit, baby. You're hurting me. Sit up."

Another giggle. "I don't believe you."

"Run your hand over your stomach," he said.

She did, moving it down sensually from her breast and stroking her skin along the way. Her hand stopped abruptly when she touched the bulge above her navel. Fingertips moved around quickly, testing and examining the hard half-globe. "My God!" Her head jerked up and she gawked down at her midsection. "You've ruptured me!"

Even though the pulled-down position of his cock ached beyond being funny, Buck couldn't help laughing, which made his dick ache all the more because of the jerks. "No, baby. You're not hurt. You just got me fish-hooked, that's all. That bulge is the head of my dick, trying to poke out through your belly."

"Yes... it is!" Helen said. "I can feel it now. Not bad, either," she muttered, rubbing her palm over the head of Buck's prick through her skin and flesh.

Chapter 11

Buck waited another moment or so, expecting Helen to sit back up and ease the strain in his aching penis. When she didn't, merely hung there between his legs rubbing the head of his organ through her stomach wall and grinning up at him, he decided to make her pay for the discomfort she caused him.

"Okay, baby, you asked for it," he said threateningly.

A grin mocking Helen's amusement spread over his face. As if doing a sit-up, he put his hands behind his head and, using only his powerful stomach muscles, brought himself into a sitting position. He grabbed Helen's hands and pulled her upright in one swift jerk. As her breast shit and flattened against his chest, Buck forced his hands into the soft meeting of calf and thigh just behind her flexed knees. He pulled her knees quickly up beside his body, and, before her feet could settle on the carpet, slid his palms down her calves and grasped her slender ankles, flinging her feet and legs out to the sides and rear.

Her heels thudded to the floor, sending a jolt throughout her body. "Buck?" Her eyes opened wide and searched his face. "Buck? What are you–" She let out a howl half of pleasure and half of fear, as the sensation of falling upward and backward caught at her sides and sent her arms and legs around Buck's body. She sucked in her breath and clung tenaciously as the room pitched and whirled about her. Then, no part of her yet touching the floor, Buck loomed above her.

With more than half of his long, black cock still inside Helen, Buck paused. He chuckled at a private thought and shook his body from side to side, then laughed aloud as Helen moaned and clung to his torso. She swayed beneath him, like a monkey clinging to a tree limb during a windstorm. Her hands were locked at the upper part of his back, and her ankles criss-crossed over the swell of his brown buttocks.

Suddenly he was no longer supporting her. She was falling to the floor, clinging to Buck and pulling him down with her. Her back thumped onto the soft carpet, partially knocking the breath from her lungs. Then, a split second later, Buck fell on top of her with all his weight, driving his big cock to the depths of her cunt as his body smacked crushingly and covered her. The air whooshed out of her lungs, leaving her weak and trembling. She whimpered, letting go and letting her arms and legs flop limply out in the classic spread-eagled position.

Straining for breath, Helen swung her head to the side and gasped, her lungs filling and pushing her tits tighter against his chest. "I can't breathe," she whined. "You're smothering me."

Buck elbowed the floor, raising his chest away from hers but still keeping her nipples in contact with his skin.

"That's better," she panted, then began to groan as he started. His ass came up slowly the first time, pulling the full length of his thick shaft out until only his glans remained between the pouting lips of her cunt. Then he slammed down into her, brutally hitting into her tender loins with all his might. It was only the beginning. He'd promised her a rough ride, and set about giving her exactly that.

At first Helen wailed and whimpered, shuddering each time he slammed his big organ forcefully up into her. He was going to kill her, she thought. He kept hammering at her so fast, so hard. As soon as she managed to catch a breath, wham, down he came and knocked it from her. It was too animalistic, too violent, like no union she'd ever had before and surely didn't want now, or ever in the future. His balls hit into the crack of her ass, time and time again, hard, splatting and stinging, chafing the tender skin. His cock seemed even bigger and harder now, as it invaded her stretched and weeping vagina with callous indifference. In and out it plunged, chafing, pulling, probing, massaging, setting her insides on fire, rubbing with such frenzied friction that she couldn't stand it another minute.

Helen was sure she'd go out of her mind the very next time Buck thrust his mighty pole up into her. He did. She didn't. It hurt. It burned. Then something inside her snapped. The burning sensation changed, slowly fusing with the pain, changing it also, the pain and the burning becoming one and tormenting her even more than before. Her guts began to smoulder. Her cunt was raw from the beating Buck gruntingly continued. She held her breath, sure that at any moment her loins would burst into flame and consume her in a fiery death.

Shuddering and moaning, she lay limply beneath the wildly humping brown body, expecting a curtain of soothing darkness to fall over her and bring with it peace and contentment. She shut her eyes to help it descend, for her to go willingly into the world beyond death, there to find relief from the unbearable heat in her pummelled, battered loins. A woman's voice caught in her ear, sobbing and whimpering. Dimly, she recognised the voice as her own. Yet it seemed apart from her, separate from her own being. Fascinated, she tuned in and listened. How strange the voice sounded, how inconsistent. At one moment it was filled with pain, the next, surprisingly, because the pain had sounded so completely unendurable, the voice whimpered with pure and unadulterated bliss. The sounds changed as she listened. The pain faded and the bliss grew large, filling the void vacated by the pain sounds.

The change was also taking place in her loins, Helen realised. Her cunt was still raw, still smouldering, but pleasure was replacing the pain. Wave after wave of intense pleasure swept out from her loins as Buck hit into her again and again. She opened her eyes and stared up with incredulity.

Sweat covered Buck's brown face and forehead. He licked at his lips, smiling and panting.

"Buck? Buck?" Helen could not go on. She sucked in her breath and bit her lip.

"Is it gettin' good, baby?"

"Mmmm," moaned Helen, through her nose, nodding her head. It was getting good, and more intense than she could believe. All her feeling seemed to be centred in her cunt. Her lips were cold and unfeeling. She bit into them with the sharp edges of her teeth. Nothing – no pain, no sensation at all. All the nerves in her body had realigned themselves, connecting her cunt and brain, sending pleasure up and down in a rapidly engulfing stream that shut out all sensation but the pleasure of Buck's big black cock stroking in and out of her screaming pussy. More, more, more, it screamed. Harder – yes... harder!

Her arms shot up around his back, pulling his chest down over her once more. She kissed wetly at his shoulder, his neck, his ear, nibbling and nipping at the brown skin as she murmured softly. The pink tip of her tongue darted into his ear and licked about eagerly. "Oh, Buck... darling!"

"Let it go, baby. Turn loose the fly," he panted.

The calves of her legs slid over his. White feet hooked under brown shins, using them as a lever to help shove her cunt up tightly against his loins. She savoured the moment, clinging to him and grinding her pelvis, feeling the full length of his big, thick cock inside her, feeling his warm balls jostling about in the crevice of her ass, feeling the coarse hair of his pubis chafe against her tender cunt-lips.

"Oh God... oh God," she moaned, clamping down her vaginal walls and caressing his organ.

"You with me now, Helen?"

"Yesss," she hissed. "Now! Fuck me... fuck me... *fuck me*!"

Danny's cock threatened to burst. He'd never seen Helen so turned on. She was out of her mind with lust for the massive black cock, hunching and groaning and grunting like a wild animal. Her face was unrecognisable, contorted with raw need, ugly. The abandoned way she thrust up to the black man sent a chill up Danny's spine. Would he ever be able to satisfy his wife after this, or would she scoff at his sexual attentions and demand more than he could give her? His mind reeled with the thought of what their future together might be like. One thing was certain: after tonight Helen would never again be the sweet innocent girl he had loved and married. He shuddered.

The sight of Buck's brown ass hunching above his wife's thrashing hips drew Danny closer. Her legs were locked around Buck's waist now, her heels beating into the cheeks of his ass. With a groan, Danny knelt beside them, getting his face up close. He watched the big cock pull out of her tightly gripping cunt-lips. The black shaft was covered with her

secretions, all wet and slippery and gleaming. Then it started back into her, folding her cunt-lips obscenely inward, drawing her asshole tighter.

Helen's moans of satisfaction excited Danny all the more. He watched Buck's cock disappear into Helen's body, heard the splat as their bellies came hotly together. It went on and on. Helen moaned and gurgled as Buck hunched frantically above her, filling her cunt with hard black meat and jerking away from her as soon as his nuts slapped into her wide-open ass.

"Buck! Hurry, Buck," Helen yelled urgently. "Yess, oh yess, darling. I can't wait for you! I'm going... going. Ouuu, mmmm!"

"Yeah, baby, yeah! I feel you coming. I feel you. You're taking me with you... baby... baby!"

Helen's head rolled ecstatically from side to side. Her eyes were clamped tightly shut, her eyeballs making little ripples under her fluttering eyelids as they twisted about unseen. "Buck!" It was a shrill scream. "Oh, Buck!"

"Catch it, baby... catch it!" Buck was straining against her now, holding his cock in to the very hilt and feeling it twitch preparatory to shooting his come inside her. He gritted his teeth and turned his head to the side, closing his eyes as orgasm took hold.

Open-mouthed, panting with lust, Danny gawked at the heavy brown balls. They pulled up slowly, tightening and wrinkling the loose skin, until they were hugging the base of Buck's organ. Helen was moaning and blubbering, already in her climax. Her cunt-lips and asshole danced and winked, her body shuddering along with the orgasmic cadence. Then the brown nuts, pressed tight against her fluttering cunt, began to jerk.

Helen's breath sucked in with a ragged gasp. "I feel it! So strong... so hot. Shoot it... in me... deep and hot! Come, daddy, come... come!"

Their mouths met in a moaning, tongue-sucking kiss. Helen's fingernails raked down Buck's back. She cupped his ass and tried to get yet more of the throbbing, spurting black cock up into her heaving belly. A tremor wrenched her entire body each time a hot jet of Buck's spiralling semen hit into the open mouth of her womb. Jerking her mouth free, Helen sobbed brokenly, begging Buck never to stop the inner inundation of her being.

But Buck could make it last no longer than the final weak twitching of his cock. Drained, his orgasm over, Buck lay on top of her writhing body only to catch his breath. Then, Helen begging him to leave it in and get it hard again, to go on with their "delicious fuck" all night,

Buck disentangled her arms and legs and crawled off her.

She caught his wrist and pulled him to his knees beside her head. "Let me suck it and make it hard," she hissed, then raised her head and took the sex-drenched, limber, black cock lovingly into her mouth.

Danny watched his wife bobbing her head, heard the lustful noises as she sucked and slurped around her mouthful of meat. His gaze moved down her sweat-soaked body, past her jiggling tits, past her heaving belly. The crisp hair of her pubic mound was now wet and soggy, clinging wetly to her skin in little ringlets. An inflamed clitoris stood out boldly in the top folds of her open cunt, still hard, still throbbing. Below her clitoris lay the yawning chasm that was now her cunt. No longer was it pure and tight, but stretched and freshly fucked.

The red of his wife's inner cunt looked back at Danny, mocking him, laughing and rolling the jets of ropy come about as she sucked hotly on the black dick that had filled her full of it. He groaned, knelt between her legs and brought his mouth to her messy pussy.

Hands took Danny's ass, positioning it. He kept at Helen, sucking at her cunt, licking up inside her as far as his tongue could reach. A pain shot up his body. He groaned and stiffened, still not taking his mouth from

Helen's hot cunt. The head of a cock popped through the tight, rubbery ring of his asshole. He whimpered, easing his ass back and letting the cock work gently up into his bowels. Soon a fat belly pressed against the cheeks of his rump. Hands gripped his hips, and Harold began fucking slowly in and out of his anus. Even more excited now, Danny thrust his tongue up into Helen's vagina and licked at the slippery walls of her cunt.

Rod came over and lay down beside Helen. Moving her slowly, so Danny could follow and continue sucking her cunt, he turned her onto her side. Snuggling up to her back, Rod reached down and raised her leg up in front of her body. Then he took her hips, pulling her butt toward him and getting her into position.

The head of Rod's prick came to her anus and pressed for entrance. It was too dry, too tight. He pulled away and aimed for her cunt, nudging between her and Danny's chin. Slowly Danny gave way, letting the cock brush past his lips and sink into Helen's cunt. It was a pleasant sensation, thought Rod, his cock moving in and out of Helen to gather lubrication with which to make the insertion into her ass easier, and Danny licking at them both all the while. For a moment he toyed with the idea of going on to orgasm that way.

But that was not what he'd come behind

Helen for. As yet, her asshole was virgin, and he wanted to be the first to screw it. Shivering with anticipation of how tight and hot she would be, Rod withdrew his rod from her warm cunt and brought the come- and saliva-wet head again to her puckered anus. His hands gripping tightly to her hips, so she couldn't jerk free, he pressed the head of his dick into the tiny brown opening.

Much to Rod's surprise, Helen made no effort to pull away. Instead, after a startled jerk at the first contact, she moaned around her mouthful of hardening dick and pressed back to help him get the head past her tight ring and on into her butt. She squealed as it popped through, then shivered as he sank it to the depths of her bowels.

Sam had been switched off. Maria, Ellie, and Bess were again sitting at the table, watching all three of Helen's holes and Danny's two being put to good use.

"Let's join the fun," Maria urged the other two.

Ellie, fully recovered now, jumped up eagerly, but begged off to catch a breather after her recent romp with Sam.

"Go ahead," Ellie said, grinning as she rubbed her cunt. "I won't be long. Let me get a little feeling back in it first."

"Okay, baby," said Maria, bending to kiss

Ellie on the mouth. "Come on in whenever you're ready. If there's not room by then, make it."

Maria and Bess moved over to the tangled mass of human bodies, intending to tangle them up more yet. Maria, being the dominant of the two, picked her spot. She jerked Buck's cock from Helen's mouth and sat on her, pinning her shoulders to the floor and bringing her cunt over her mouth.

"That's it," Maria crooned down at Helen. "Lick it. Get your tongue up inside and suck me for all you're worth."

"You rotten bitch," Buck said to Maria. "That blow job was beginning to feel pretty good."

"I can do it better," Maria taunted, opening her mouth and flicking her tongue. "Come on, Buck, put it in here and go right out of your mind."

Buck grinned down into her face. He put one foot on the floor behind Rod's head and eased the other out until he stood straddle-legged with his cock in Maria's face. "Get it, baby," he said softly. "Don't bite me when you come, you hear?"

"Or what?" Maria asked, licking at his glans and cradling his balls in her palms.

"I'll finish in your ass, if you bite," Buck grinned.

Maria wanted no more of that. The one time he'd stuck that thick pole in her rump had caused her to bleed from the tear. "You won't even know "I've got teeth," she promised, then opened wide and tugged him into her mouth by his balls.

Bess looked frustratedly about for a suitable spot. Danny's cock was the only one free. But his position would permit sucking only, and she wasn't hot enough for that yet. However, she did want to join in the Helen-centred orgy. Harold's fat ass could stand a little thrashing, she decided, turning and going back to the table for a quirt. It always made her hot to lash him as he buggered one of his boys, and he liked it, too. His climax was always so much more gratifying with his buttocks striped and glowing warm at her hand. "What are you gonna do?" Ellie asked, when Bess picked one of the two quirts from the table.

"Warm my old man's ass," Bess replied, swishing the quirt through the air for drill. "Wanna help me?"

Ellie nodded, picked up the other quirt, and followed Bess back over to the maze of writhing bodies. She'd never liked Harold. Once the bastard had slipped up behind her when she'd been kneeling and sucking Rod, and before she knew what was going on his pudgy belly was pressing against her, with his dick rammed painfully up her ass. She welcomed the opportunity to even the score.

The left cheek of Harold's plump bottom going to Bess and the right to Ellie, the two women set about raining blow after swishing blow onto his white tail. It didn't remain white long, for they went at him with obvious pleasure. The leather thongs whacked over his trembling rump, turning his whole rear into a pink glow, with red welts appearing where the straps themselves had bitten. They kept him hunching furiously into Danny's wavering body, letting him pull out before both whacked the quirts against his reddening buttocks and sent him lurching forward with a howl and planting his peter up Danny's shit-chute once more.

"Mmm... mmm... mmm," fat Harold crooned, shoving his stick all the way up Danny and bending over him as orgasm flooded over him.

Bess and Ellie beat his ass all the harder, neither trying to keep a cadence now that Harold was spewing his come and moaning with ecstasy. All their strength was put into the thrashing of those quivering, jiggling, fat globes of virtually hairless male butt. On Ellie's buttock appeared a few drops of blood, and she caught herself, quitting before Bess did. She was even with Harold now bringing blood to his tail was further than she'd intended to go. It was enough.

Reversing the quirt, holding the thonged end in her hand, Ellie roughly shoved the handle up Harold's ass. She pushed it all the way in, until the strips of leather dangled from his butt like wet and drooping tail-feathers. Standing back at a short distance, she surveyed her handiwork, unable to quell the roar of laughter that burst from her at such a ludicrous sight.

Fat Harold's orgasm was the first, and it seemed to set off a chain reaction. His come spurting up into Danny's bowels pushed Danny over the brink, and his unattended prick began a solitary dance, sending his semen gushing out and falling to the carpet. In his excitement, Danny sucked down with all his power, drawing out the nearer folds of Helen's much-used cunt into his mouth and chewing on them with lip-covered teeth.

The harsh suction was a completely new sensation for Helen. It felt like her insides were being pulled out into Danny's mouth, and once there being eaten and massaged in such a delicious way. She wailed a muffled wail up into Maria's hot cunt and let herself hurtle into orgasm at Danny's mouth.

Rod gritted his teeth. Helen's virgin ass was the hottest and tightest he'd ever had the pleasure of putting his dick into. Now, added to that scrumptious warmth and snug fit, her anus winked and fluttered about the base of his fully planted rod. He'd wanted it to last longer, and tried to hold back. But it was useless. Helen's spasmodically clamping asshole and the heat of her inner body was too much for mortal cock to endure. She milked the come right up from his balls. He joined the chorus of moans, and inundated her bowels with a surging stream of spurting, hot come.

Hearing the others go into orgasm one by one triggered Maria's release, especially when Helen sucked down ecstatically on Maria's pussy and reached up to squeeze her breasts at the same time. Maria's hands pulled Buck's big cock down into her throat and she gurgled the beginning of her climax around it. She cupped her palms over the tightened cheeks of his ass and held him to her face, taking most of his gigantic pole down her throat and swallowing around it over and over.

The ringed portion of Maria's throat flicked maddeningly over Buck's big organ. He stared down in disbelief at her hollowed cheeks and protruding lips. The red lips were still working tightly and softly around his shaft, trying to take the rest of it inside her oral cavity. He groaned, grabbed the back of Maria's head, and, already shooting come, pulled her face toward him till her lips mashed into the coarse pubic hair.

*   *   *

Helen lay on the floor, a fatuous smile covering her lovely face. One hand lay weakly over her ultra-sensitive vulva. The fingers of her other hand probed testingly at her expanded asshole. She was completely oblivious of t he others, who were standing around her in a circle and watching her reaction.

Bess licked her lips and tore her gaze from Helen. Putting her mouth close to Maria's ear, she whispered, "Let's play darts."

"I'd intended to," Maria said softly. She and Bess had made the darts together after Maria had dreamed up the little game. "I forgot all about it, Bess. It's getting late. Maybe we'd better wait till next time."

"You promised, Maria," Bess accused.

It was true, she had confided her plan for Helen's initiation to Bess, and had given her word that Bess could toss the first dart in return for helping her make them. "All right. It might revive us all. Get the straps."

Bess hurried off and came back with two chamois-like strips of leather. She pitched one to Maria, then knelt at Helen's feet and tightly bound her ankles together, while Maria set about lifting Helen's arms up over her head securing her wrists with the other soft leather strap.

"What the hell are you doing?" Rod demanded.

"We're gonna hang her from the ceiling and throw darts at her tits and fanny," Bess excitedly informed him.

"Like hell we are," Rod shouted. "Untie her."

"Rod," Maria said softly, cajolingly. "Come on, honey. It won't hurt her nearly as much as that ramrod of yours stuck up her ass did. Get the darts, Bess. Show him what they're like."

Again Bess hurried off, this time returning with a large lidded glass bowl. She stopped in front of Rod and lifted off the lid. Maria reached in and pulled one of the tiny darts from the alcohol-soaked sponge, where the points of all the darts were embedded.

"See, Rod?" Maria asked, passing the dart to him. "It won't be a bit worse than getting a shot at the doctor's."

"Well, I'll be damned," said Rod, breaking into a smile at the tiny torture implement he held between thumb and forefinger. "Matchsticks and needles?"

"Yes, and paper strips inserted and folded to serve the place of feathers. We put a lot of time and work into those things," Maria exclaimed. "It'd be a shame to let them go to waste."

"Hm," said Rod, "damned ingenious." Then he lifted the matchstick dart up to his chin and flicked his wrist, sending it flying straight for Bess' tit, and hitting her directly in the hole at the end of her nipple.

"Ow! Goddamn it, Rod, what did you do that for?" Bess whined, doing a little Indian-type dance as the dart sagged from her skin without falling free. "Pull it out. I've got my hands full," she told Maria.

Maria jerked it free and stuck the needle point back down into the alcohol soaked sponge. "Okay, Rod?"

"Sure, baby. Where do you want her?"

"Put her on the hook. It ought to be about the right height."

"Now stop it!" Danny broke in. "I can't let you do that!"

Maria, again grinning her evil grin, took a dart from the sponge. She turned to Danny and, hiding the dart from sight, took his limp organ in her other hand. She held his glans between thumb and forefinger, then brought out the dart and jabbed the needle into the head of his penis, it all happening so fast that Danny didn't know what was coming.

Yelping with pain, he wrenched free of her

and pulled the needle from his organ. He started at her, as if to jab it into her belly.

"Danny!" barked Maria, stopping him in his tracks.

"Remember what happened to you at the beginning of the party? Shut up, or I won't be as easy on you this time." Maria smiled, then added with a tinkle of laughter in her voice, "Have you ever had a knitting needle stuck up your cock? Cross me again, Danny, and that's what I'll do to you."

Danny backed away, his head shaking and his eyes wide. His face looked like he could feel the knitting needle just from Maria's threat. Maria laughed and hurried to join the others, as Danny sat down as far from his wife's swaying body as the room would permit.

A bewildered Helen hung from the ceiling hook, whimpering and looking wildly about. Her toes dug at the floor in an effort to raise her body high enough to unhook her hands. It was a futile effort, for only the very tips of her big toes could make contact with the carpet, and then not firmly enough to do anything but cause her body to twist and turn helplessly.

"Should we blindfold her?" Buck asked.

"What are you going to do to me?" Helen's voice was edged with terror. "Oh God, don't whip me... not like this."

"You want a blindfold, Helen?" Maria calmly inquired.

It made Helen think of an old Foreign Legion movie. It was all so unreal, she the one being executed, and Maria the captain of the firing squad. She shuddered, and shook her head. "No, don't blindfold me. What are you going to do?"

The bowl now rested on the floor. Maria bent and took a dart for each hand. She aimed one of them for Helen's breast, and sent it flying.

Horrified, Helen watched it come at her. It dropped short of its mark and stuck into her upper stomach. She screamed out and wrenched her body, the leather strap biting harder into her wrists as she turned jerkily about. Then she gasped aloud, hunching forward as a second dart hit its mark and stuck into the left cheek of her trembling ass. "Oh Lord! Don't throw any more... please don't hurt me."

"We've got almost a hundred darts here, Helen," Maria told her. "You wouldn't want us to waste any of them, now would you? Don't be so inconsiderate."

Another dart hit into the back of her right thigh. Helen groaned, but made no verbal protest. It would do no good to beg. Maria would become all the more excited if she begged. So she hung limply from the hook, closing her eyes and feeling dizzy as her body jerked and twisted. One dart after another pricked her skin and dangled like a banderilla from a weakening bull in a Spanish arena. They would not kill her, as the matador did the bull, of that Helen was sure. It was little solace, however, as the endless darts embedded themselves in her flesh painfully. She moaned and groaned almost constantly, jerking involuntarily and twisting as each new dart found its place and bit sharply into her.

The waiting was the worst part of all. As the game progressed, Maria had assigned differing points for each part of her anatomy. The players were taking more careful aim now, and recording their scores after each shot. Helen wouldn't look. She kept her eyes clamped shut and tried not to wonder when the next dart would prick into her flesh. But she couldn't help but anticipate the next dart, especially when all got quiet. She knew someone was taking aim and involuntarily tensed her body for the stab of the endless supply of needle-darts. When it hit, sometimes in her breast and sometimes in her buttock, she'd yelp and wrench her torso, despite her resolve not to show any feeling whatsoever.

Blood trickled down from her punctured tits and buttocks, candy-striping her white skin obscenely. She looked like a peasant girl in an old torture dungeon, a picture from right out of the dark ages. She knew this, and it humiliated her. Her body hurt all over, the physical pain fusing with the psychological pain and causing her to weep bitter tears over the atrocious manner in which they were debasing her.

All was quiet for an exceptionally long time, then she heard Maria announce happily, "I won," and knew that all the darts had now been thrown, that almost a hundred of the dreaded little things were hanging from her flesh. The voices came closer, then one by one the darts were pulled from her body. It was worse than when they'd hit into her. She hung as still as possible, whimpering with pain as all the darts were withdrawn from her.

The last dart was finally gone, she knew. Why didn't they take her down? Why? Then she knew. Beginning at knee level she felt tongues, two of them, one in front of her body and one behind. She opened her eyes and saw Maria kneeling before her, her tongue darting out again and again, licking every trace of blood from her skin. It was Bess at the back, she saw, doing the same. The tongues were doing more than simply licking her clean of blood, they were beginning to drive her out of her mind, as well. The closer they came to her cunt and ass, the more Helen sighed and gave herself over to the incessant lapping.

Bess' tongue moved over her buttocks again and again, licking the dart-inflicted pinpricks as a mother lioness would lick her wounded cub. It felt good, soothing, healing. Then fingers parted her buttocks gently, and Helen moaned with pleasure as Bess' warm, wet tongue slid up into her asshole and licked about. And Maria's tongue, now in her vagina, sending a chill of pleasure all over her body and making her break out in goosebumps. On up Maria licked now, over her belly and each tit, until Helen was screaming from the pure delight of it all.

Both women ceased their licking as Rod approached with a can in his hand. Maria and Bess backed away, making room for Rod to move around Helen's body. He shook the can, then began to circle her as he sprayed the white froth from her neck clear down to her ankles. He opened her buttocks, putting the can to her anus and spewing it full of the substance.

When he filled her cunt with the cool foam, Helen was sure she'd pass out. God, it felt good, hissing and gushing up into her vagina, filling it to overflowing and then oozing out and running down the insides of her thighs. Finally the can was empty. Rod stopped. She heard the can hit off at a distance, where he'd tossed it. Then he was calling to the others, "Come and get it. Dessert with whipped cream topping.

Let's lick every drop of it off sweet Helen."

Then tongues were all over Helen, licking in unison at her tits, her legs, her back, her stomach, her ass. It was enough to drive her out of her mind. She quivered and moaned, trembled and jerked, coming again and again as all those tongues kept loving every inch of her body.

A mouth attached itself to her ass and sucked the whipped cream from there. Then another mouth covered her cunt, lips forming tightly and sucking the cream from her fluttering vagina, going up in after the last traces with a hot, probing tongue. The rest of the tongues kept at her, licking her all over as she shuddered in ecstasy from the simultaneous ass and cunt tonguing. It was too much... too much!

An orgasm like Helen had never before experienced took hold of her. It began in her cunt, but didn't stop there. It spread to her asshole, making it join in and quiver with delight. Then the rest of her body was flooded over, twitching, jerking, thrashing about. The waves of orgasmic pleasure seemed even to wash out into her fingers and toes. It turned her to jelly, a writhing, blubbering mass of jelly.

Tremor after tremor shot through Helen, making her buck and jerk like a psychotic receiving electric shock therapy. She screamed out loud and long, her face mirroring the unbearable sensations going on within her, then she slumped into a dangling, used-up female form, swaying unknowingly from the hook, unconscious.

Chapter 12

It was Friday night and the moon was full shining down brightly from a clear Georgia sky. Danny Nielsen hummed happily to himself as he turned off the main street and headed for home at ten p.m. He'd had two appointments that evening, and had sold them both, a $10,000 straight life policy to the last, and a $5,000 endowment on a new baby at the first one.

The old touch wasn't gone, after all. He still had it. The knowledge made him doubly glad, for these were the only policies he'd sold all week. Ever since that damned party, six days ago, he'd been worried sick. His guts had ached so badly at times that he was sure he was developing an ulcer. Helen's strangeness had kept him upset, unable to think about anything else.

The party had done something to her, changed her somehow. All Sunday, the day after the party, she'd kept to her bed, getting up only to go to the bathroom occasionally, not even bothering to eat. She wouldn't talk to him at all, except to give him a sharp "leave me alone," when he tried to cheer her up. And during the week it was little better. The housework went undone for the most part. She seemed to have no interest at all in making a home for them any more. He suspected that she was spending her time with Maria, the daylight hours that she had to herself. He'd asked her about it several times, and had gotten nothing but an enigmatic smile for an answer.

And sex, or rather the absence of it, had crushed him most of all. Helen wouldn't let him get near her, let alone touch her. She'd never treated him that way before, never. Right from their honeymoon on she'd been eager to see that he got all the loving he wanted. Even when she wasn't fully in the mood, why, she still gave herself gladly and seemed to enjoy the fact that he found satisfaction through her body. But not this week.

The goddamned party had changed all that. After Sunday she was civil to him, but insisted on a hands-off policy until, as she said, "I regain my sense of balance and perspective." It had been torture for Danny, living in the same house with her and not being able to touch her, kiss her, hug her. At night, lying side by side in bed, that was the worst. Like brother and sister, he'd thought, and knew that it couldn't go on that way for long.

But now, now it was over, and Helen was coming around. What a difference there'd been when he came home for supper. The house was neat and clean again, like a home, like their home had always been. He'd known then, the moment he walked in the front door, that Helen had found her balance, that she was once again his wife, that things would be right between them.

In the kitchen, she'd smiled sweetly at him and left her work to warmly embrace him, had poured him a cup of coffee and sat him down at the table to await the meal. They'd talked, neither of them mentioning the party or the days since, while she added the finishing touches to the dessert. He'd watched her, beaming as she moved about in her frilly dress and open-toed sandals. She was the old Helen once more, the sweet, angelic girl he loved.

After supper he'd apologised for having to go out and keep the two appointments. She didn't mind, she told him, and had walked with him to the door and out to the car. She'd leaned in the open door and kissed him, telling him not to be any later than necessary, that she had a surprise for him when he got home, one that she knew he would like. He'd wanted to know what the surprise was. She wouldn't tell him, but did give him a hint. He'd find the wife he wanted waiting, she'd promised, then added sultrily, "It'll be a night you'll never forget, darling," before she shut the car door and hurried into the house.

Now, as Danny pulled into his driveway, he felt a stirring in his loins. He stopped the car and cut the lights and engine. Glancing at the house, Danny saw that only one light was on, the one in their bedroom. His heart beat faster as he opened the door and climbed from the car. Helen was waiting for him in bed. He could picture her lying there in her sexiest nightie, smiling at him as he stood admiring her from the doorway. She probably had drinks already made and waiting, too.

The handle of his brief case felt slippery as he walked across the lawn toward the front door. Switching it to his other hand, Danny wiped the sweat from his damp palm on his trousers. He took the three steps in one leap and reached for the doorknob, turned it and went into the darkened living room.

"Helen?"

"Back here, darling."

Her voice was edged with excitement. Danny broke into a smile and set down his brief case on the floor, deciding that the paperwork inside it could damn well wait till morning. He shrugged out of his coat and pitched it toward the half-seen couch, then, loosening his tie, went down the hall toward the bedroom.

Abruptly, Danny halted in the open doorway. The smile faded from his face. A tremor shot through his body. He gasped in horrified disbelief. "Oh no, Helen... no," he groaned.

There was Helen, his wife, standing in the middle of their bed. Her face wore the evil smile that belonged to Maria. A skin-tight black leather jumpsuit covered her body, with cutouts leaving her firm breasts and entire crotch area naked. High-heeled lace-up boots were on her feet, and a whip was coiled in her right hand. Her legs were spread wide apart and her hands rested on her leather-covered hips.

"Do you like it, Danny?"

He shook his head dumbly, unable to speak or tear his gaze from the obscene sight.

"Well, get used to it," she chuckled. "You're going to see a lot more. This is the new me... and I love it!"

"Helen?"

"Yes, Danny?"

"You're not serious, are you? Tell me it's only a joke."

Her smile broadened, and her eyes

squinted down to slits. Reaching out with her left hand, she motioned for him to come, at the same time letting the whip uncoil like a snake until its thonged tip lay on the floor, waiting...

THE END

THE END

Just a few of our many titles for sale...

EVELINE

Gorgeous nymphet Eveline embarks on a dizzying path of sexual encounters as she tries to satiate her urgent needs on as many men as possible. Vania Zouravliov's rich and vibrant drawings bring explicit life to this unparalleled story of teenage debauchery

GAMIANI

One of the most important novels to have come off the 19th-century presses, this novel explores one night's abandon by the Countess Gamiani, her lesbian lover and a voyeur turned protagonist. Shockingly explicit, even by today's standards.

FANNY HILL PT.1

The world-famous Erich von Gótha turns his limpid brush to the most famous erotic novel of all time to turn this first part of the insatiable Fanny Hill's adventures into a beautiful production. Hardback with dustjacket.

BEATRICE

Beatrice narrates the story of her own initiation into the pleasures and pains of the flesh in this exquisite tale of incest, sodomy and sexual awakening. Stunningly illustrated by Lynn Paula Russell.

Eros and Thanatos

A high-art treatment of hardcore subject matter, this book contains the stunning work of late artist Klaus Böttger. Sex is lovingly, graphically depicted as bodies writhe at the very pinnacle of ecstasy. Contains two short novellas.

The Lost Drawings of Tom Poulton

British erotic institution Tom Poulton completes our trilogy of his work with this set of drawings that were previously thought to be lost. Also contains one of the dirtiest short stories, illustrated by the artist, the EPS has ever published.

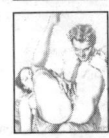

The Secret Art of Tom Poulton

The first in the series of Tom Poulton books, this is a must for any erotic library. Containing some very graphic illustrations from this master of his craft it shows Poulton at his orgiastic best. Also contains two period novellas.